THE STORY OF KETH

An attractive blend of poetry and humour.

The Cork Examiner

Lady Girouard wafts us into a world of fancy which keeps us wondering and delighted to the end ... It is a story that fascinates a reader, and it is told with rare literary grace.

The London Quarterly Review

Blanche Girouard's bitter-sweet little tale, in its whimsical Irish setting, is a perfect example of its rare and charming kind.

The Liverpool Post

Blanche Girouard has an exquisite manner, and her imagination is sensitive and vivid.

The Universe

It is a thing of beauty, the beauty of pure language, of poetic thought, and of idyllic imagery ... The book ... will delight the lover of letters. For here is writing of a purity and restraint which is rare and an imagination which is ever at play...

The Brisbane Telegraph

THE STORY OF KETH

by

BLANCHE GIROUARD

introduced by

DR MARK GIROUARD

SANDNESS
MICHAEL WALMER
2020

The Story of Keth first published 1928

Introduction first published in this edition
© Mark Girouard 2020

This edition published 2020 by

Michael Walmer
North House
Melby
Sandness
Shetland ZE2 9PL

ISBN 978-0-6486909-3-1 paperback

INTRODUCTION

My mother, Blanche Maud de la Poer Beresford, was born on 13 October, 1898. She was the daughter of the 6th Marquess of Waterford, and was named after her two grandmothers, Blanche, Marchioness of Waterford, daughter of the Duke of Beaufort, and Maud, Marchioness of Lansdowne, daughter of the Duke of Abercorn. The Beresfords had come to Northern Ireland in the early seventeenth century, and in 1717 Sir Marcus Beresford had married the daughter and heiress of James Power, Earl of Tyrone, of Curraghmore in County Waterford. The Powers of Curraghmore became the most powerful of the many branches of the Power family, which had come to County Waterford in the fourteenth century and had flourished there. They may have been of Norman origin, called Le Poer, but the name was soon changed to Power. It was romanticized without any justification to de la Poer by the de la Poer Beresfords from the eighteenth century onwards. They were Protestants, and carried great weight in the Protestant Church of Ireland; but my mother became a Catholic after she married my Catholic father.

She did not go to school. She was educated by governesses, and up to her marriage spent most of her time in her family's Irish homes, Curraghmore in County Waterford, and Glenbride, a shooting lodge in the Wicklow mountains. The 'demesne' of Curraghmore is of great beauty, arguably the most beautiful in Ireland. It is encircled by a stone wall at least ten miles long, to form a little kingdom, pierced by the fast-flowing River Clodagh (or Cleodagh), with an amphitheatre of woods rising to sheep-walks on either side of it, opening out on the west to the Comeragh mountains. The house at the centre of this has an entrance forecourt 500 feet long by 192 feet wide, lined on either side by stabling for 100 horses, built of rather grand architecture in the eighteenth century. It leads up to the original tower house of the Powers, behind which looms the square mass of the house that was added onto it. The tower is prominently surmounted by a statue of St Hubert's stag, with a cross between his antlers, the crest of the Powers. Just across the river from the house were the kennels of the Waterford Hunt, virtually a family hunt, of which the family took turns to serve as MFHs (Masters of Foxhounds). My mother and her sister Katie were joint MFHs from 1923 to 1926. But although she loved hunting the country round Curraghmore, and described hunts vividly in some of her writings, I think that she was happiest walking or riding round the local farms or the little houses of the 'mountainy men' in the Comeragh and Wicklow mountains, and looking in for tea and talk round the peat fires in their dark and friendly kitchens. She had the gift, which everyone who knew her commented on and loved, of reaching out with the same warmth and interest to everyone she met, whatever their age or background.

There had been troubles between Irish landowners and tenants in the Land League days in the 1890s, but much of the friction was removed when, by a series of Land Acts, the tenants acquired their freehold from the landlords. Even so the 'bad times' of the war for Irish independence, followed by the final fearful year of civil war between Irish Republicans and Free Staters were difficult for Anglo-Irish landlords, with their many links to England. The Cork Republicans were especially notorious for burning down country houses. In 1922 Curraghmore was saved from likely destruction when a body of well-disposed local republicans, who had taken over the forecourt buildings, refused to let in a Cork contingent when it came marching up the drive and demanded admittance. My mother, unlike the rest of the family, felt sympathy for the idealism of the best Republicans, and wrote movingly about it in letters at the time.

She had been writing poetry for a good many years before embarking on *The Story of Keth*. She was writing this when she and my father, to whom she was engaged, were taken over in 1927 to Coole Park, to visit Lady Gregory and Yeats. Yeats read them his poem 'The Tower', and gave her a signed copy of it, and Lady Gregory gave her a signed copy of her play *The Story Brought by Brigit*.

When *Keth* came out my mother sent it to her, and got a long and charming letter back, saying that she had started to read it, and had been unable to put it down, and had read extracts to Yeats when he came to stay, and how much he had liked it too.

The Story of Keth was inevitably compared to James Stephens' *The Crock of Gold* and *The Demi-Gods,* and their influence, not always for the good, cannot be denied. But what distinguishes my mother from Stephens, who was a Dubliner born and bred, is that she knew the countryside she was writing about, and the people in it, and was able to write about land and people with the vividness of personal love and knowledge – especially the mountain lands around the Wicklow Gap, where *The Story of Keth* starts and finishes, and the gorse-coverts and little towns of County Waterford. I love her description of a country fair and circus in the rain on the green outside Dungarvan, and the woman at the stall with her wailing cry "Try … yer luck in coppers".

I did not see all that much of my parents in my childhood. My sister and I lived, ate and slept on the nursery floor of a big London house, presided over by a difficult and possessive nanny. But my times with my mother were lovely when they took place. She would come up to the nursery on Shrove Tuesday and toss pancakes with us before the nursery fire, or take us for walks and tell us wonderful stories, or as a treat let us come down to breakfast with her and my father and eat fishcakes together. On holidays in Ireland we went out in the woods with her to build ourselves houses of bent boughs and leaves, or she would take us visiting in the little houses around Glenbride. When I went off to my first boarding-school in September, 1940, I have a vivid memory of her, very tall, standing on the platform at King's Cross Station in London, waving as the train drew out. It was the last time that I saw her, for she was killed in a car crash a week later.

MARK GIROUARD
London, November 2019.

To
MY MOTHER

CONTENTS

CONTENTS

PROLOGUE

THERE was once an immortal who came to live with men. For her heart was grown weary with the shadows, the dim songs and the gentle winds of those regions of enchantment that lie between heaven and earth. Straying into the land of mortals, she found that there the rose-petal was soft to touch; that sap flowed there into the curled leaf and into fruit where teeth might pierce and sink; and that strong men were there also, whose limbs were not fashioned of such stuff as would melt upon a breath of wind.

So she stayed on the fair earth, and tasted and drank of each delight of which it is possible to conceive. There was no whim she did not satisfy, no play invented of humanity she did not sample. Yet withal she remained a stranger among men, since she would share neither in their toils, nor in their sorrows. For she said: "I will not bow my head in the service of any man, else shall I be bound to earth and become as other mortals, that must grow old and die."

Now of every possible disaster, she could imagine none so great as that she should die. For in her wanderings she had found one only whose grief might touch her heart. And that one was herself.

It came about after a great while, that she had exhausted the more common sources of delight. She had run through wet grasses after rain. She had eaten hot peaches, sun-embalmed on a red wall at noon. She had ridden intrepid horses. She had seen the sun set and the moon rise; and on every one of these occasions, she had had at her shoulder the companion she desired. She had been hated of a hundred women and loved of a hundred men. And she had been told she was beautiful in the language of youth, which is to worship; and in the language of middle age, which is to cherish; and in the language of old age, which is the giving of gifts.

PROLOGUE

When she had tasted all she might, she bethought her that she would return to that kingdom whence she came; but that land now seemed pale to her and cold. So she began to seek out new ways with which to divert her mind on earth. It is said she grew skilled in many charms and in the spells that are written in old books, so that she could play with men's minds as with a box of toys, and with the elements as with a candle.

One time, men said, she learned the tongue of beasts that she might call them to her when she would. She would steal the sheep-dogs from their folds, and command them with so mischievous a skill that the sheep were mingled upon the hillsides, till there was scarcely one but ran with some flock other than its own. On bright nights, it was said, men's hearts grew cold to hear the small sound of their baying beyond the little glens. And when the shepherd would set out at daybreak to fold in his young lambs, he must tramp forlorn on the long hill: till by and by his dog came crouching to his feet, bedraggled and full of shame.

Or they told how she took a fancy to another's child, and stole it from its people. Some say that she took it because it was so small; others, that its very ugliness amused her, because it had red hair and was freckled like a sheep. Yet having captured it she did not know what to do with it, for the deep thoughts of a mother were alien to her heart. She would play with it carefully, as if she feared that it might break; and sometimes she seemed to weary of it, and would treat it without gentleness. Nevertheless she spared no trick or scheme that should provide it with food and shelter; and did she suppose that none was near, she would treat it with such overwhelming affection that it began to cry. Some say that she tired of it at length and returned it to its mother; others that it fell sick and died, at which she was overcome with grief. Indeed, it were impossible to tell if these tales were true or false, so lightly did men's fancy roam who had looked upon that fair strange face.

Yet these freaks and idle fancies contented her only for a little. And as she tired of them one by one, her heart was filled with an immense weariness, for she said: "The world grows old to me and out-worn, like a song that is sung too often." At length she was come to such a pass, that her joy seemed without spice or flavour, did it not occasion in some other an equal measure of distress. The innocent delight of youth would sting her to unreasoned anger, men's commonplace content filled her with distaste. She would wander idly through the world and, choosing from among men the most noble and proud of spirit, bring them with swift strokes to her feet; but seeing them there, she grew indifferent and left them where they fell, their quick pride broken in the dust. Her name grew to be a terror to all that heard it, for they said: "Let a man but look upon her, and she will make of him a piteous slave."

It was from Ireland—where is the gate of the Immortals—that she began her travels. For a hundred years, she wandered in many lands. Then she grew lonely. And coming back, she had no wish to travel further; for the furze was gold upon the ditches, and on the little hills, and the wind was soft upon her cheek. In the world,

she had been known by many names.   But
here she was named Kethlenda; till one or
two, dreaming it day and night, grew weary
of that long far name, and called her Keth.

I

JUNE

It was June by valley and hill. The wind flew on a glad voyage. The river leapt towards the sea. Dark underneath the forest, the sky saw in a million bluebells the shadow of its face.

The river sang and the wind. From treetop to treetop, birds sang of a quest not unavailing, and of an end but just hid beyond the hill.

In the midst of this light, this movement, Keth walked knee-deep in bluebells, yet in her step there was no direction and no joy. She carried a switch of willow in her hand; and as she went she struck at the flowers in idle sport, till there stretched from behind her a white trail of stalks gaping headless, of flowers hung heavy on thin threads and dark flowers lost upon the ground,

THE STORY OF KETH

The child of some poor man—its little body scarce concealed in tatters of clinging cotton—followed her at a short distance, staring at her with huge eyes like some frightened but fascinated rabbit.

"Lady," it said.

And at that it hid in panic at the sound of its own voice, suspended like a thin squeak in that immensity of colour and sound, and peeped at her from among the fern.

But presently: "Lady," said the little voice, "look around at what you did."

"If I should turn back," said Keth, "it would put a spell upon you, and you would be turned into a twig or a dried leaf. Did not your mother tell you that?"

But still the little one remained.

"Lady," it said, "they have their heads drooping. And there is a rent in their stalks the like of a finger that is cut." And on its face the grime was parted of two tears.

Keth gave a little laugh.

"I will not look back," she said. "For if I should see that ruin, it would make me sad. And it is a pity, child, to be sad."

And she strode on the faster; till growing

weary, the child turned back into the wood, and forgot in some small play of its own the tragedy of the flowers.

Presently she reached the bridge of Ooler, below which there blinked in the sun a little coloured house, and an old man on a chair before it who, meditative, fished for trout. He did not catch any fish. But the garrulous brook was at his feet, and he was well content.

The Immortal watched him for a while. Then she began to throw stones into the water, for she liked to see how he would start in trouble and surprise, thinking that a fish had at last come to that stream.

Now it happened that a Saint of Heaven rode that way. He came by singing a little song. It was a song without time or tune, or indeed, any reason whatsoever; for the song of the light of heart is as the song of birds that wanders idly without care.

Keth looked upon the stranger. Yet having looked upon him, she saw no further than his eyes.

For these eyes were a calm sea.

They were the sun of winter and the shadow of summer.

They were a port where little ships might rock gently in a deep place.

And seeing them, she was filled with misery because she had been throwing stones to trouble the calm of an old man. And it was not the old man she pitied. But herself.

Yet in a moment her grief was turned to anger. For "It is not right," she said, "where the hearts of all are without peace, one to be thus indifferent and still." She came out upon the bridge, and began to address him with soft glances and beguiling words.

Now though she had lived long, the years had left no print upon her face. On her cheeks was still a tender bloom. The colour of honey was in her hair, as it brushed her little ear like a moth's wing, or curled its delicate tendrils on the pale curve of her neck. The light of storms and of summer nights was in her strange wild eyes. And as he looked upon her, she seemed to him at once more beautiful, and more sad than any he had ever seen. Then he remembered his people, among whom he would labour day and night on the dark bogs and the desolate hills. "I cannot stay with you," he said.

At that she bowed her head, and with her cold cheek laid to his beast's shoulder, besought him that he would not leave her.

"I cannot stay with you," he said sadly. And putting spurs to his horse he rode away.

Then the Immortal bit her lip with rage. And she declared that come what might, she would follow after that Saint of Heaven, till the song in his heart was turned to bitter gall.

As for Cleran—for so the Saint was called —three nights he lay in sore perplexity. "I could not stay," he thought. And again, "Who am I, that I have passed her by? Am I not a Saint of Heaven, to heal the weary of heart?"

Then in the love of his people he forgot her perilous cold cheek.

II

MORNING

THE Saint slept. While on the dim bogland, the Saint's horse stood with his tail tucked in and kept watch over his master.

He was such a creature as will attach itself, by heaven's gentle law, to the sublime of spirit. He was a cynic, a base realist, a hard-headed disciple of reality. He had a high back, and that stood for competence; a nose delicately aquiline, which would butt its way where the august had quailed. His brow was of an intellectual vastness, his ears sat far back upon his skull in a carefully concealed disdain. He looked on men with a cold eye. He did not consider them ornamental: they began life with a certain grace, yet ended it with the walk of a crow; they worked without joy for fifty years, and in the end achieved only an apish exterior and a profound unhappiness. For himself he was fond of thistles, philosophy and sleep. Sentiment he abhorred.

Cleran had purchased him but lately from a tinker in Ferns. When the tinker bade his horse good-bye, he had rubbed him on the back of the neck and called him a "divil." Of which endearments the horse, looking back from the corner of his cold eye, appeared to be unconscious. At this his master rubbed and pinched him with a greater violence, whereat the creature arched his neck, laid both ears tautly backwards, and gently bit him on the arm. Thus did they show their affection for one another.

The tinker had named him Meleanthus. For he said: "If you have a good horse, you might as well call him by a sounding, tasty sort of name, and not just any common lump of a name like José or Tommy or Bob." So he sought out an uncle of his own, who would travel the roads with the weight of learning in his head, and impart it to the curious-minded in the shade of a little ditch [1] or wall. And it is from him he got the name of Meleanthus.

[1] In parts of Ireland the banks are known as "ditches."

THE STORY OF KETH

It was daybreak. The sky was still, yet full of movement—the movement of a grey light which flowed in, silently, almost imperceptibly, from the Eastern limits of the world. Over the dark hill-sides a cloud slid by on velvet feet. It was desolate.

Cleran awoke. His spirit came unarmed out of sleep; and perceiving at its door the imminent strange day, it shrank within itself for fear.

At that he rose to his feet. And bowing his head upon his breast, he prayed:

"O Light, O Silence. My radiant one, spring of my heart's joy, come into this empty house.

"The grey fog of night lies thick in the long passages. The windows are yet unlit. O my Beloved, draw from the earth the trailing mists, and touch this impotent heart with gold.

"The day waits. And yet I do not go, because you are not with me. I will not tarry. I will go if you will come with me.

"You have wrapped your cloak about me. The fretful swarm of little cares cannot trouble me any more, the perilous unknown day is without power to pierce this aureole of gold.

"You will sing to me upon the mountain. Through the dun ways of toil the frail note of your song will follow me.

"Through light, through dark, you will be at my shoulder—my laughter in sad company, my still place in the tumult of crowds.

"O Beauty terrible and swift, you have come to rest in the small space of my heart."

At that he turned his face to the grey dawn. And having saddled his horse, he rode upon his way.

Nothing stirred. Before him, over hills monotonous and rounded, little roads dipped or climbed into the sky. In a patch of crooked fields the houses stood silent, as it had been in a valley of the dead. Yet even as he looked, there came from one chimney a timid thread of smoke. Presently, at a little distance, a similar blue thread rose straight into the air; till from each house was sent out this signal that its charges were come safely out of sleep, and stirred to the small tasks of day.

Then the Saint put spurs to his horse and pressed on the faster. For it was his custom to ride from dawn till dusk by the lonely and the desolate ways, giving judgement among men, and healing with his quiet touch the sick in body and in mind. He kept, moreover, a little store of gold, that the unfortunate might not ask in vain. For it was said that he had once known hunger and the rack of grief, and that in his gentle heart these things were turned to an infinite pity of the world. Now he was rich, yet without splendour; he was a king, yet without pride. As for food and the night's shelter, of their love the people would give him these; while they counted it a reproach did he depart without the means of refreshment for his journey. So that of his own he had nothing, but a rug of yarn, lest the night overtake him upon the hill, and such vessels as are required for the setting out of a little meal. For if he should eat upon the roadside, it was his delight to share that meal with friends.

Presently he passed a house where the mortar was fallen from between the stones. He checked his horse and, dismounting, stood upon the threshold.

Within he found two who had grown very old. The man sat with stooped frame upon the bed—for there was but the one room—while the woman, who was as frail as he, hobbled hither and thither in a deep concern as she bent to her work about the house. The hearth was beautifully whitened with a piece of chalk. She had cut out bright pictures and affixed them with pins in a zigzag pattern upon the wall. In a corner were three shelves, beautifully garnished with papers scalloped at the edges. And there was nothing else.

"Now come in an' welcome," said the woman. "Though indeed I'd be shamed to ask you. The place to be so tossed. I do be frettin', to think will I have it shwept, and proper, and settled nicely, so I do. . . ."

"Your house is beautiful," said Cleran.

At that the old man stirred, and great tears began to trickle down his cheeks.

"Don't be fretting now, you poo-r cratur," said the woman—and she wiped away his tears with her apron. "He is crying," she said to Cleran, "because he has lost the use of his limbs."

"Then who is it," said Cleran, "that will bring bread into the house?"

"There is a little field of grain," she said, "that he was sowing, before the use was taken from his limbs."

"And will the little field keep you for the winter?"

"That is as God wills," said she. "For there is none to reap it."

Then Cleran took off his coat, and went out to reap their field of grain. As his keen blade brought down the yellow corn, and divided it from among the rocks and the quicken-trees of the hill-side, his spirit was comforted. When all was cut he bound it into sheaves, so that by evening ten stooks stood in a row between the crooked walls. Then he returned into the house.

The pot was already among the ashes, and when he had shared their dish of tea, he took his leave. "To-morrow," he said, "I will bid the miller send up his cart from Ballymore, and you shall be paid for your corn."

"The blessing of God be upon you," said the woman, and she followed him into the doorway. "Yet you must excuse us," said she; "the place to be in such a fright. . . ."

And turning back into the house she began once more her troubled wanderings, moving a pin here and a cup there, till it seemed he had faded from her mind. "I do be fretting," she murmured, "to think will I have it shwept, and proper, and settled nicely, so I do. . . ."

Cleran continued on his way.

Before long he passed another house, from whose doorway there came to his ears the murmur and the growl of rage. Within he discovered a long man and a little woman with fawn's eyes. It seemed they were quarrelling together. Yet as he looked upon them there fell on their spirits a great calm, as the sunlight at evening time will fall aslant across the world, till the birds grow still among the trees. In this gentle light they looked on themselves for the first time, and considered the reason of their words.

"What grief is in this place," said Cleran, "that you darken it with the shade of anger?"

"It is this way," said the man. "She doesn't like me, and you can't get away from that." And he nodded his head and sighed deeply.

"That is so, mister," said she. "Now in all the ring of the world, you couldn't find another man does so dissatisfy me as that man there."

"She has the like of an aversion for me," said he. "My voice is a trouble to her ears, and if she will happen to look at me, she doesn't like it."

"It's this way," said she. "Now if I was a little ass, and had to keep on looking at a shtick: or if I was a young pig, and had to keep on looking at a pan o' grease: or if I was a great king itself, and had to keep on looking at another king—it couldn't give me more displeasure than I have to be looking at himself."

The man considered her mournfully. "She's such a little woman," he said. "You would be surprised at the words that would come out of her."

And with a melancholy satisfaction, they surveyed the hopelessness of their position.

"How long are you married?" said Cleran.

"Three years it is," said she, "since the match was made between us: I to bring him the farm, and he to bring me forty pounds. And it's long enough since he spent that."

"And were your hearts married on that day?"

"They were not then," said he: "only to be fettered together like a pair of tin kettles on the tail of an ass and cart."

"Then I pronounce your marriage null and void," said Cleran. "You are free to leave for where you will, and as for her, she need look no more on the unpleasant prospect of your face."

"That is right," said the man. And he nodded his head in a deep gloom.

"You had best get your property together," said Cleran, "and set out upon your road. For if it is good to do a thing, it is good to do it quickly."

"That is right," said the man. And going to the settle he brought out a tail coat, two coloured handkerchiefs, and a small mirror with a sunset painted across the corner.

"Fetch me my shtockens from within," he said to his wife. And she brought him those.

"Now fetch me the half-plug of tobacco that is beneath the pillow of the bed."

The woman brought him the tobacco. She was so small, that she scarcely reached above his elbow. She tilted up her head, and a tiny doubt was in her face.

"Arrah now leave your codding," said she.

"Isn't it your wish," he said, "to see me quit beyond the gate?"

"Arrah, go 'way now," said she. And she poked him in the chest with her thumb.

"You said," he told her, "that you didn't like me."

"I couldn't spare you," said she. "Wouldn't the house be quiet in the morning, and you gone away?"

"You said," he told her, "that you would sooner a clucking hen for company."

"I couldn't spare you," said she. "Wouldn't the tongue be shtuck in to me palate with the want of use?" And she began to laugh uneasily.

Then suddenly she put up her hands, and drawing down his head to hers, she covered it with violent kisses.

Then the Saint of Heaven turned, and went upon his way.

MORNING

The sun shone tenderly upon him. In the light of evening he turned aside into the bogland, and rode apart as was his wont. For in that hour, men said, when the light grew red upon the hill, there rode at his side one who was tall and shining, and talked with him there. Not that the mountainy men had seen this thing. But when he came down, they said, his face was full of light, and the strange brood of dreams was in his eyes.

But to-night he had gone only a short way, when he came upon a little lake that was set in the bogland like a jewel. On its banks the feet of many children darted in their silent play. Their little thin legs were browner than their curls, their eyes flittered hither and thither like the timid glances of wild things.

Cleran rode among them. "You must be careful," he said to the children, "or the king will come out of that little lake and call you to the Kingdom under Wave."

The children ran about his horse, and curiously touched its silken coat. "Is that so?" whispered they.

Then Cleran loved them.

"Come to me, my darlings," he cried—
and he slid from off his horse—"and I'll tell
you of the Kingdom under Wave." As
they ran to him, his arms enclosed their
little bodies, till their soft ribs sank in
beneath his hands.

He sat in the rough heather and told
them strange tales of knights, and arrogant
queens, and palaces of limpid jade. "The
flowers in that place," he said, "are like
curled snakes and the fluttering wings of
doves. The princess of whom I told you
brought one back to earth, but when she
looked at it again, it was but a snail's shell."
And as he spoke he believed these things
himself, because the children were so sure
of them. Indeed they would forestall him
in his words. For if he thought: "The princess shall have pale hair," they were immediately telling him as much; and if he would
have said: "Her eyes were blue," they had
already informed him that these eyes were
the colour of forget-me-nots.

At length he must reluctantly take his
leave. But as he mounted his horse they
called to him: "And are you too after the
Princess?"

MORNING

Cleran said that he was not, but that you might meet a princess at any time, and that was why the world was so nice.

At this they shouted at him all together.

"Is it by the Togher road you are going?"

"That is my way," he said.

"Then she is gone up only just before you," they cried. "And there is no doubt she is a right princess, for her hair is the colour of honey, and she is as proud and as scornful as you please."

At these words the peace went from his heart. And in its stead there leaped up a great flame that was neither of the sun, nor of the moon, nor indeed, of any celestial fostering.

I I I

EVENING

THAT evening as he rode with tired limbs across the bogland, he heard the voice of a woman singing. And looking up, he saw her to be but a dim speck upon the road before him. Yet her voice came to his ears in a thin, clear stream till she had put a ridge between them. For it was still.

Presently he drew near a solitary farm. The quiet of evening fell about it as a bird falls, closing its two wings. The patient cows moved in slow procession to their milking. The flowers, that huddled from the mountain storms between a little paling and the wall, were turned in the dusk to pallid moths.

As the traveller approached, some one lit a light beyond the window. And he thought: "The day is dead now," For that orange square was at once the centre and home of all desire.

Meleanthus too was thinking. And his thoughts were: "The quality of the hay will be good in this place."

He therefore turned in at the gate without being asked to do so, and, drawing up at the door that his master might knock easily, he dropped one ear and waited. Cleran knocked. And immediately was heard the sound of chairs creaked back across the floor, as those within were disturbed at their evening meal.

The people of the farm gave him a great welcome, for it was not often that a Saint of Heaven crossed their threshold. They took the pack from his stiffened shoulders, and led away Meleanthus to his quiet stall.

Now as he came into the light, he saw the form of a young woman sitting over the fire. She did not raise her head, but there was no mistaking the curls that grew upon the nape of that neck. Then he knew the meaning of the dusk, and of the light in the window. And his heart was filled with an infinite content.

They drew up a chair for him to the

table, but it did not face in her direction. And when they had put hunger behind them they began to talk pleasantly to one another.

There were a number of people about the table. There was a faded woman whose voice, too, was faded. There were children that crept like rats about the table-legs and the hearth. There was a man whose laugh was like the voice of a hen when she is insulted or terrified. And whenever he spoke the others would excuse him, saying: "He is innicent," or "He is like a little bit simple." There was a wise and oracular man who did the honours of the house. It seemed he was some hired man or poor relation. And there was a timid, dull man to whom none paid any attention. He was the master of the house.

As for her who sat above the fire, not one of them spoke to her or made mention of her at all, for it seemed as if they feared her. But behind the words of Cleran there was her only.

"You had rain on the road to-day, sir," said the wise man.

Cleran said that he had not, and that it was a strange thing how the rain would fall

in one part of the hills and not another.
But his thoughts were: "If my chair had
faced in her direction I could not well have
looked at her, for my inquisitive gaze must
have called forth hers in return. But now
I can see her dim shadow as it stretches up
the wall, and half-way across the ceiling:
so that I must be aware should she but turn
her head."

"No doubt," said the wise man, "it is
terrible dirrty weather: but that is the Will
of God, and you couldn't tell what would
be in His head at all. Now if it's drowned
the world itself He did, it isn't you would
know what scheming and contrivance was
in it, for the ways of God are very deep."

"Near drownded I was in the night,"
shrilled the man whose voice was like a
hen; "going from the cowshed to the house,
and back to the cowshed again, where a nice,
souple, butty kind of a calf is this minyit
upon the straw."

"Isn't it queer now, sir," said the faded
woman, "that sort to be created by God
Almighty so lively and so sensible, the time
a child is still as it were a trouble you'd not
leave from your sight at all."

"You might say," said the wise man, "that the ways of God do be something shockin'."

"Now the small one I have here," said the woman, "isn't it wake as a wet rag he is yet, and he a care and a toil to me these seven year." And holding the child against the warmth of her body, she stroked his yellow hair.

Then Cleran felt a great tenderness towards her, as he did that night to all the world. "They have you worn out, the little troublers," he said. "But whatever may be done for the child, I will do it in the morning."

"He have the like of a twist in his stomach," explained the master of the house. "But thank God, it is only a middling small twist." And that was the one word he spoke all the evening.

"Now that's another remarkable thing," said the wise man, "the little sickness is in this country, and the wealth is in it, since you came to it yourself, sir."

"Sure, it's you are the light out of heaven," said the woman.

"Not," continued the other, "that it's all

would be content. But indeed, what is it they would be doing if they were not complaining. Sure, if the Lord sent down a shower of silver, it's a shower of gold they'd be looking for after.''

"Yet time was," cackled the innocent, "when they hadn't that would buy a jacket for a gooseberry.''

Their words were a delight to Cleran. But his thoughts were: "Her hair was pale beside the river. But to-night it shines with twenty little flames."

When the meal was finished, they went to sit around the fire: yet none would go near to the stranger, but sat always a little apart from her as if they feared her touch might burn or harm them. She sat with chin in hand, so that the shadow of her arm lay like a red stain upon her throat. When the flame of turf leapt noiselessly, that shadow too leapt noiselessly upon the whiteness of her throat.

Now all asked for entertainment, and the innocent took down a fiddle from a peg in the wall, and scraped merry jigs upon it with a yellow-haired bow. All gave high praise to his playing, so that he hopped hither and thither with delight. If he had possessed a wing he would have trailed it upon the ground.

Next the company turned to Cleran and begged that he would tell them a story. He hesitated for a moment. Then he promised to do so. At that they settled their faces into the lines of profoundest thought, for there was not a story of his but contained some hidden wonder.

Cleran said: "There was a king who had many palaces, and great was the care upon his shoulders. Yet in the love of his people he found a quiet joy.

"It happened one day as he drew homeward when the sky was pale, that there sang to him a little singing bird from among the dew-wet leaves. And as he listened to that song, his own life seemed to him an outworn and a senseless thing; and himself no better than a wayfarer, or a wandering star that has shone only on drifts of knocking ice.

"Then the bird ceased. And his heart was left troubled in the silence, for he could put no meaning to the song.

"Now as he came out of the night into his palace, the lights greeted him with a peculiar splendour, and in the crackling fire was a radiance he had not known. There was meat set upon the table, and this too seemed to him a thing beautiful to consider. He fell to thinking of the hands that had set it there. 'They are strange to me,' he said. 'I do not know if they are soft or white. I do not know if they are cool, and with long tender fingers. And so it is in whatever palace I will rest.' And he thought: 'It were very sweet if the same hands should set the cloth at each day's ending, and range the bright dishes upon it, and stretch out with a welcome for my body when I am come in from the dust of the road.'

"As he thought thus, the song returned into his mind. He heard again the brown singing bird, deep in the dew-laden, heavy leaves. And her meaning was no longer hard to understand."

At that there was a little stir through the company for Keth had raised her head. Yet she did not speak, but stared still before her into the red turf.

"For was not this your meaning, O sing-ing bird? 'He that has many palaces may be looking still for the home of his own heart. He that is beloved of twenty thousand, may be looking still for the love of one?''

Then Keth began to speak: and her voice was like a low chord struck in the heart of every listener.

"That was no timid song of homes, and of wiving, was sung by the wild bird of the forest. But a song of love only, of flight, and the shattering of chains." She gave a little laugh, and the room about her was numb and held still with fear. "Let the king leave his palaces and follow the tawny singing bird. For that is the true end to every tale!"

Cleran answered: "If the wild bird would come to him for shelter, the king would care for her tenderly. Not one delicate feather of her wings would be broken or crushed. His love for her would be like the little rains that bruise no petal of a flower."

He ceased. But though he waited a full minute, she did not answer. Then he turned to the listeners.

"I will tell you now the end of the story:

and if it is not an end, then all ends are but a beginning to the tale that will follow after. The bird is yet in the forest. The king is yet in his palace. For his people are dear to him, and he would not leave them for a song sung in the night for the boldest of singing birds."

At this the company nodded wisely.

"Indeed," said the wise man, "that's a real, palatable tale."

"Oh—now—wouldn't ye be crazed listening to it," sighed the lady of the house.

"I cot a bird o' Monday," chuckled the innocent. "And if he sang me a song of sixpence, it's t'ree penn'orth is shtuck yet in his gullet!"

For search as they might within their heads, not one of them could make head nor tail of a word that had been spoken.

Now all—with uneasy sideward glances at the stranger—talked of retiring for the night.

The wise man set out for his own home. And outside, the stars were seen to commune with mists of earth in an ecstasy unaware of men.

The Mother, an arm alert to protect her little ones from harm, piloted them across the hearth. Two candles burned upon the wall. She took one, and led them down a step into the inner room. Boards creaked and a shadow bounded to the rafters. The door closed.

A cold blast shivered through the outer door. Then the master of the house arose, that he might know all was well with his cattle for the night. Fetching a lantern from the shelf, he took down the nodding candle. The light of the room fled to him from every corner and, surrounding his form with radiance, passed with him out of the house. You could see him going down the hill, where the candle winked—a little star—beneath unnumbered constellations.

The room was silent. Then the man who was like a hen arose with a silly chuckle and went out after his master.

There were those two only, and the fire-light. A sod of turf fell in and a weak flame licked it without noise. From the inner room came vague stirrings.

Then Keth spoke.

EVENING

"When you came in out of the twilight, although I did not see you, I knew how your tired limbs sank into the chair that was waiting for you.

"I knew when you stood close to my shoulder, or when the pitiful length of the room was stretched between us.

"When the food was before you, and a blast of the hot steam touched your lips, my own two lips were scalded and in pain . . ."

Behind the looming hearthstone, crickets were singing to one another.

"To-night," he said, "I held out my love to you and you would not take it."

And she answered: "You would surrender me your love. But you would surrender nothing else." And rising, she crossed the room quietly, and passed out into the unknown night.

The light of the candle returned, and with it the master of the house. The innocent wavered at his heels.

"Who was it," asked Cleran, "that sat here at your fire?"

"I'd not answer you as to that," said the master of the house. "She came in, and she is gone back now, please God, to her own people. It was no good thing, she to go by me in the darkness of the night." And when he had bolted the door, they turned each to his own bed.

So darkness settled upon the farm. The mother slept, yearning over her children. The innocent slept across a knotted dream. Cleran did not sleep, for the dusk was become for him a mockery, the light in the window a delusion. And out upon the hill Keth trod with anger in her heart.

Only Meleanthus stood munching in the content of true philosophy. For he had long ago banished all dreams, aspirations, and idle imaginings as troublesome, unnecessary, and without sense. While the quality of the hay was such as could not be denied.

IV

THE COUNTESS

Iᴛ was early, and the world was empty but for a frost that cracked and shifted. Eastward the sky paled wearily, as if loath to embark upon another day of sorrow. Sometimes, in the solemn hedgerows a leaf fell limply to the ground, its life departing through the motionless dawn.

Cracked Lal Corrigan peeped from a house that had no windows, and ventured into the silence, dipping and peering. Some hens, ruffling their feathers in the dust of the yard, lifted their heads and stared at her. She caught up her skirt and ran at them, and they fled with terrified screeches. Reminded by the fowls' curiosity of her defenceless position, she returned into the house and, fumbling in deep secret places, disinterred an axe. She also placed upon her head a little hat of purple velvet, and taking from a jug some shining beads, she stroked them gently with one hand and arranged them about her neck. Thus reassured, she set out with a sense of bravado into the high road, singing little snatches of ₁song while she brandished the axe joyously. And the song that she sang was:

> "I am the Countess Corrigan
>   Of high blood and ancēstry,
>   Jewels hanging from me
>   Like cobwebs from a rafter.
>   If ye'd see a fine knacky sprout
>   Of th' ould Irish gintry
>   Look at me now!
>   And take off your hats from your heads."

Presently, upon the road behind her there crackled the sharp sound of wheels. She gripped her axe the firmer. Yet she kept her head, behaving in all things as became a woman of quality. The wheels came clanking and shrieking up the road. Conscious that at any moment great deeds might be required of her, she began to sing at a great speed:

THE COUNTESS

> "I am the Countess Corrigan
> Of high blood.
> Mansions I have in the North
> Stocked well in the manner of gintry,
> Hunters of all sorts,
> Fox-dogs and hairy tarriers . . ."

Then there drew abreast of her a little ass and cart. A man walked at the ass's tail. His hand fell upon its back with a faultless regularity, while "G'wan-away-out-o'-that!" said his voice, as if it had been a clock ticking. At every fourth step he beat the ass. And the first step of that animal was swift, the second was without enthusiasm, the third was weary, and on the fourth she would have stopped altogether had it not been that she was hit again.

The Countess dipped aslant towards him, and whispered to him confidentially. "Isn't-it-tirrible-cold?" said she.

She spoke always in whispers—save when alone.

He swept off his hat. There is no doubt he was a man of intellect, for his face was crossed and furrowed—squeezed, gathered and pulled crooked—by the pressure of imponderable thought. But in the midst of this ruin his eyes frolicked, like a pair of kittens in a churchyard.

"Indeed, yer ladyship," said he, "you never spoke a truer word."

The Countess panted with delight. "High and low, high and low, Micky Quailey," said she, "isn't it the same for all?"

"That's it," said her companion. "Now only a while since I ris' up, and I says to meself: 'Will I go walk,' I says, 'before I takes me breakfast?   For where is the sense,' I says, 'to be stoppin' for me mornin' coffee and the frost that is at me in the bed like rats at an apple?' "

"Is it in a bed you slep'?" whispered the Countess.

"A soft bed, but a contrary bed," said Micky.   "For it's nettles that was in it."

The Countess plucked at the jaunty tatters of her dress, while her head darted hither and thither in sudden jerks.   "Did you hear," she whispered hastily, "who it is does be lodging at the bridge?"

"Aye?" said Micky.

"Isn't it the blessed saint of hiv'n and no other?"

"Arrah that one," said Micky without

interest. "Don't I know him better than the heel of my own toe?

"For all that," he pondered, "you might be acquainted with a man, and you might not know him at all. Now that sainted man of God, hasn't he a nice face, but you couldn't tell what was be-hind it."

The Countess trembled with emotion.

"Shame on you, Micky Quailey," whispered she. "A man has God resting in his heart like honey in a flower."

"I was speaking with one," said Micky, "is working at Tim Healy's of the Glen— a weighty gallous man has a power of words in him would blasht the truth out of a tinker—and he said to me: 'You might be a saint to-day,' he said, 'and to-morrow you might be only a middling harmless kind of man; and as for the day after, it's by then you might be swappin' lies with a devil unbeknownst.' "

"Sure that one has no thing in his head but the clack of his own words," said the Countess in a fine disdain.

"But I ask you," said Micky, "is it a good thing, or a proper thing, one the people has fixed and settled nicely as a saint, to have took up with—who they say?"

She drew nearer.

"Wasn't it at Tim Healy's," whispered she, "SHE was first seen?"

"That is what he said. 'And for why,' says he, 'was the high saint colloguing in that place, but to be telling her riddles through the night no Christian man could know the sense of?' "

The Countess turned her eyes inwards, and searched in the scrap-heap that was her mind. Then she put her mouth close to his ear. "Would you say," whispered she at a great speed, "is he breaking her to the ways of God?"

"Well, if he thinks he's doing that, then the thought is in his head and the wish is in his heart do no more resemble, than water does resemble drink."

"But it's a true saying," said he, "that there's nothing like holiness to confuse a man. Now an honest, thieving kind of man —if he seen a hatchet, he'd call it a hatchet, and if he seen the like of a coumerade, he'd say: 'That's a damn rogue.'

"But do you see now, a decent poor man

the like of that man there, if you told him the nature of this ass he'd say God made it, and if you shown him a thistle, he'd be telling you it's a bloody flower."

The Countess thought for a long time.

"You might say," said she, "isn't it them durrty little thistles is the bane of all?"

"Now that one there," said Micky, and dropped his voice until it creaked, "Don't you know, and don't I know, she to be one is of the ancient blood?"

"There is nothing like blood," cried the Countess Corrigan. Speaking thus on a great theme to all the world, she forgot that she was not alone. "A terrible thing it is, tormenting you day and night with high dreams and lofty as-pi-rations, roaren' and leppen' in the pate like butter in a stew-pan."

"Blood is all very well," said Micky, "but I would sooner a bit o' land or a nice cow.... But I'm telling you. If it's once he spoke with her, isn't it twenty times? Gaming with her in the noonday, stringing her long lonesome tales upon the brink of night. I'll tell you, it's follying him she is: and un-the-less he'll put a curse upon her, won't she have him in the end of all?"

"And did you see her since, yourself?" whispered the Countess.

Micky put his hands into his pockets. And at that the ass thrust out her head and stopped stark in the middle of the road, as if her machinery had run down.

"It was a rough night," said he. "The wickedest night ever fell out of the heavens with rain. I was going up be the Gap Road when I seen before me a great light beyond the ridge of the hill. 'What's that?' says I. 'Will I go run?' says I. 'You will not,' says I. Then I seen the brink o' the Gap. And I seen the rain falling. And didn't she rise up athwart the hill in the likeness of the risen moon?"

"Well, now, aren't you the man did see great wonders in the world?"

Micky spat meditatively. "Many things I done," said he. "In France I was one time and I seen the King of France driving in his state and splendour. Six little mules he drove, had their carcasses striped and spotted like fishes of the sea."

"Do you say that?"

"I served a black king," said Micky, "and a white king, and a savage king had ten rings did hang out of his face and a pelt of hair upon his arums. . . ."

For a while he pondered upon this. Then he continued his tale.

"Well, I seen her there upon the road. Then I ups and I stands there—quiet like —the head cocked as it were jaunty, do you know, the way she'd see I didn't mind her. And—'There are hills in the North and in the South,' says I, 'do tremble at your name. There are men of honourable estate—prelates, magis-trates, poten-tates——' "

"Good fer you," cried the Countess, and she clapped her hands and laughed delightedly.

" '—Are kilt with dread of you this day. But if I'm no great shakes itself, it isn't only one saint or two do have me for their pet and their delight. So if ye have any evil intention,' says I, 'the way ye'd be ashamed to be where y'are, Go!' says I.

"At that there went the like of a tremor through her bones, and she let a screech out of her, and didn't she run from me like a deer across the ridge o' the hill."

The Countess placed her finger on his coat, and addressed him very quietly. "Is that a woman," said she, "is coming before us on the road?"

"It's a woman it is," replied Micky with an equal quietness, "if it isn't more than a woman."

"Is it 'that one,' do you think?"

"It might be that it is," said he.

"Will you speak with her, do you think, or will you leave her quiet for the wonst?"

"Tell me now," said Micky. "Is it o'Monday to-day, or Tuesday?"

"I think it's Sunday it must be, for last night I seen Danny Fitz, and his mother had the collar on him the way he'd be ready for the Mass."

"Well, now, isn't that a terror? For if there's a misfortunate day in the calendar of the week will bring me no luck nor fortune, it's Sunday is that day.

"But tell me again. Was it a dark girl we passed in the heel of the gateway a while back?"

"It was not. But a low-sized dwarfish little woman with a foxy pate."

"Well, now, isn't that a fright? For if there's one thing brings bad luck on a man, it's to be crossing with a foxy gerrl the time he'll go abroad out of his bed.

"But tell me again. Is it a rabbit is stirring in the gripe?"

"It is not then," whispered the Countess; "but a big rogue of a hare, and the eyes of your buried da, or your mamma maybe, that are looking from its head."[1]

"Well now, isn't that a fright?" said Micky. And he scratched his head in a deep thought.

"I think, maybe," he said, "we'll not trouble her this day. For where's the sense in being dead when you might have lived to rock the world?"

At that he directed his mind towards a deep bohireen, that was hardly now in its prime, for the rocks had worn through it as elbows through their sleeves.

He laid hold upon the ass's bridle. "Gwan-away-out-o'-that," said he.

The body of the ass swayed gently backwards, while her neck grew to so great a length that it seemed it must break off in the middle.

Then she surrendered wearily. And in a little while the cart was rattling and bumping out of sight.

[1] In parts of Ireland the souls of the dead are said to inhabit the hares upon the hills.

V

DEFEAT

The sun had risen. The earth was no longer thick with rime, but glittered in a thousand jewels—each jewel a drop of dew on a bowed blade. There sparkled from each tiny face the ultimate red ray of power, the infinite green ray of peace. And in each that restless or profound energy, travelled long years out of the sun, found rest for its unquiet courses and was perfected for a little space.

Keth came swiftly up the road. Once in a while there rose in her throat a little laugh, as if it had sprung there of its own volition. The world was grown young again and budded in her path. It was cold. It was keen. It sang to her. "You are beautiful," it sang; "none can withstand you." For though the jangled commonplace of love grow weary in a while, yet to be loved of a Saint of Heaven is new as a new day.   While the pursuit and capture of a saint, was it not worthy of her shaft; since there were arrayed against her not only the pride of one poor head, but all the mountainy men of Wicklow, and beside them the company of heaven, stooping from their sapphire thrones and whispering encouragement?

Her road left the soaked fields.   The silent mist of the mountain fell about her way.   From the heather intricate with dewdrops, the chucking grouse poked up their heads and talked of love to their hidden mates.

Shadows came near out of the mist.   The shape of a hare sat up, listening, then delicately dropped its paws to earth and cantered away in a long stride.   A shadow, colossal, mammoth-like, loomed upon the hill.   Then that monster emitted a thin bleat.   It shrank, grew tremulous, was shaken into many jewels.   And the tiny feet of a sheep came pattering across the road.

Another shadow grew before her.   It was high as a mountain.   It was lean and full of angles. Character was in every line of it, yet character of so perverse a nature that each line was at variance with its neighbour, each stroke a denial of the stroke which should come after. Thus in its bowed head was a humility belied by the braggart swing of its heels. Its shoulders drifted in the sky, yet its feet fell punctually to earth without error, and without illusion.

Now at this vision there occurred that in Keth for which experience had no name. The blood went from her wrists and from her knees. The breath went out from her body, yet was caught as it were within her throat, where it seemed like to choke her. Then the mist divided. And there bore down upon her Meleanthus—one ear cocked forward in readiness for all the world might bring, the other laid back upon his neck to show his actual disdain of it. In his care, the Saint of Heaven rode out into the world.

Meleanthus perceived her immediately. Yet he continued with an even gait.

For his thoughts were: "The ninth time you meet a girl by chance is the time you shouldn't notice her."

DEFEAT

"And in our position," said he, "you can't be too careful of your company."

As for the Saint, he was not immediately aware of her, for his spirit walked in a place apart. He thought upon the Seraphim who guard the ultimate steps of the throne of heaven. "Such purity," he said, "is beyond the imaginings of thought. Thus and thus," he said, "shall their heads droop. Their curved wings meet above the throne as in the dark sky North meets South, as West will touch the hem of East."

Then he saw Keth. And the angels perished from his heart.

"How fair a dawn," he said, "that brings you first into my way!" And he looked tenderly upon her.

"This morning," said she, "as I came up the road, I passed a rabbit in a snare. Go quickly, Saint of Heaven, and set it free."

"I do not know," he said, "if you are laughing at me. But indeed I would speak with you awhile."

At this Meleanthus stretched his rein, and drew cunningly towards the edge of the road where there grew a pleasant piece of grass. For he said: "There is no doubt we shouldn't be here. But if you're in a bad place, and there's good grass in it, you shouldn't leave the grass behind you."

"It grows late," cried Keth. "Already the old men await you. And at their milking the girls press their cheeks to the warm cows, remembering your smile."

Cleran considered her.

"I am troubled by your face," he said. "It is too sorrowful."

At that she drew near the horse, till with her fingers she touched the rein upon its neck. But the good horse only browsed the faster; while now and again he twitched his skin, as if he were annoyed by some pestilent kind of fly.

"Indeed," said Cleran, "I am sore perplexed because of you. Many times I have left you to walk among the people; but while I speak with them your face returns to me, as it were a blade turned in my heart.

"How shall I choose," he cried, "between my people and your face?" So deep were his thoughts, that he did not perceive how her glance was made beautiful for him alone.

"Yet what," he said, "am I to each, but a lamp going by upon the road? For has not each one his own care—the man, his field and the helpless cattle that follow him for food—the woman of the house, her children with their little hands? But you have nothing, but the length of the world and your sad heart."

"Saint of Heaven," said she. "You are not looking at me."

"Can it be," he said, "that the one is greater than the all, and the love of all a poor scattered thing and a cry squandered to the earth and sky?"

"You will not look at me," she said.

"Shall not there come to each one care? And if that *one* seem to him beautiful withal, if her eyes are a trouble to his thought, and the turn of her cheek is a terrible wonder to break the quiet of his sleep, is it for this that he shall turn away? . . . Why did you laugh?"

"Look into your heart, holy man. Is it pity that is in your heart?"

The mist divided, so that the sun came royally and shone upon the hill. The chucking grouse talked merrily of spring.

"For shall he love well," cried the Saint, "who shares no ill? If she be despised, shall not he be despised also? If men look at her askance." . . .

At that he met her eyes. And as he looked into her eyes his voice died in his throat, for he thought: "I speak but empty words."

He turned away his face.

"You are right," he said, "that it is not pity I feel for you. It is rather pity which will bring me back to my poor people, that I had near forgot."

"You will not go back!" she said. "But you shall be my one love from this out, by strange roads and dark arrogant seas; and we'll tread the careless ways of Spring, and whisper soft things in a field of grasses when the scythes are sharpened on the hills."

"It is too fair a dream," he said.

"And we will watch the night from a still place, till we are full of scorn for the fate of kings, and pity for the lonely moon."

Now the Saint was troubled beyond measure.

"Alas," he said, "can we not cheat the net of fate? You shall walk with me among the people, and be my comrade and my bride. They shall not call you an ill name."

At that she seemed so still that he turned to see her face.   It was distant and terrible.

She smiled. "Shall I follow at your heels," she said, "and watch you gentle to another?   Or shall I share your task, so that men will say: 'She is not the Saint, but she has caught a little of his splendour.'   And I shall earn a smile from my lord, maybe, and a kind word at the close of day."

Cleran gathered up the reins.   "We have said enough," he answered.   "It is a pity we should say too much."

As the horse stirred beneath his heel, she clutched the rein.   "You shall not go," she said.   But he cast her roughly from him and rode in haste upon his way, till the untroubled mist went by and hid him from her sight.

She stood where he had left her.   There was a small pain in her finger where the rein had grazed it.

From beyond a curve of the far hill, the hoof-beats stirred tenderly and died.

Then the grouse resumed their silly chuckings.   And the blatant sun shone without cease on the rasping tin-kettle of the world.

V I

SILENCE

It was after this that the Saint of Heaven fell
sick of mind. For wherever he went, the
thought of Keth would follow him, blight-
ing all else. The fair orderly estate of
Heaven wherein, with the stars for company, he had bowed his head and walked
content, vanished from about him. He was
a jangled string that filled the earth and sky.
He said: "If I meet her now I will go by
quickly. I will not look her way." Yet at
each turn of the road he thought: "It may
be that beyond the bend she will be waiting
by a little wall, with her wan face." His
soul stood wounded and alone. He was
immense. He was terrible. He was a dis-
cord that drowned the harmony of worlds.
Heaven and the infinite stars were less
great than the pin-point that was himself,

He reasoned in his heart. "When I loved God I was at peace. I walked by the pure light of joy. In this love is neither peace nor joy. Yet, do I look to Heaven, I would not return. It is grown impotent to me and far. It is grown pale as the moon beside a little fire of sticks."

It seemed to him, did he walk among the people, that he perceived on their face a similar disquiet. At this he would question them, and in his eyes was a helpless and pitiful entreaty. "My children," he would say, "what is your trouble? Am I grown strange to you that you look so curiously upon me?"

"Indeed," they answered, "we've nothing against you. For weren't you always a decent, quiet, harmless poor man? And don't the people like you very well?" And they looked upon the ground.

He remarked, too, that some who had hitherto fled his sight—the cunning, the evil, and those who lived by obscure means—now came to solicit his protection: and this at first caused in him a deep distress. Yet he thought: "Who am I, that I should turn away? For have not I sinned also in my heart?"

Now as winter was spent and turned to spring, there fell on the valleys a heat ill-matched to that season of the year. Where Cleran passed, the roads were desolate; and did a stone roll from the horse's hoofs, it fell with an unseemly clatter that remained long in the memory.

Riding one day where the fields grew scarce towards the Gap, he met a man who had his home beside that solitary road. His chin was grey and rough as a burned hill-side. He did not seem to lift his feet, because his boots were ill-laced.

"Come on up now," said the man, "for I'll thank you to do a little turn for me."

Cleran answered without haste. "It was not your custom, Maurice Finn, to come to me asking advice."

"It was not then," answered he. "But it's how they're saying, that one man must help another; for aren't we all poor sinners, God spare us, will meet the one judgement in the end of all?"

There are some in whom boldness is a splendour and insolence a song of joy. But this man was brazen without ease. He was insolent without delight.

"Listen," said he. "Won't you say a word to the people? For indeed they're not civil to me at all. And if they could do me a hurt, they'd do it surely."

"It has been said," answered Cleran, "that smoke is but the child of fire."

"Now I'll tell you the truth," said Maurice Finn. "There was a day when a little curse slipped across my tongue; and didn't the man I spoke to go die on me from that hour, and I with no wish in my heart for him but that he'd be running and leaping till the end of time."

"And did he die?" asked Cleran.

"Well then isn't he dying on me yet? Not that the curse was a wake curse. But that's a tough man they say, and none that could have touched him only my-self."

"I will come up," said Cleran. "And we will speak with the people of this thing."

"Hurry now," said the man. "For there will be thunder before long." And they set out upon the still white road.

Presently they saw a woman who ranged this way and that upon the hill-side, seeking her cows. Her feet made no sound among

the heather.   Her great hat and the tatters
of her dress were coloured like the hill.

She dipped behind a stack of turf.   "That
is Moll Higgins," said Cleran.   "When she
comes near I will speak with her of this
thing."   He watched the stack.   A turf-
sled lay derelict beside it.   Two minutes
passed, and she did not come.   Then he
saw her going quickly from them around
a curve of the far hill.

Presently, coming round a bend, they
heard the croak of a cart-wheel where a lane
of stones was sunk between two fields.   Two
mountainy men were going home, after
bringing their store of flour and of yellow
meal out of the town.   He heard their mur-
muring speech beyond the wall.   The gate
from the road still swung upon its hinges,
but when the cart stopped, a smallish dark
man came back and shot the bolt.

"Those are the sons of Nan Corrigan,"
thought Cleran.   "They will wait for me at
the gate, for they had always a great welcome
when I came.   And it will not be hard to
speak with them of this thing."

But when he came to the gate the lane
was empty.   Out of sight, he heard the cart

bumping on the stones that here and there had fallen in from the two walls.

Before long they left the fields behind them. When they had gone a mile or more, he saw at the roadside a rawboned horse in a red cart. The shadows of a woman and two men went back and forth upon the bog-land, for they were cutting rushes at a little distance and bringing them to the road upon their backs. Though they were near at hand he heard no sound. But from across the glen he heard, between two cliffs, the clatter of a stream which came to him on a drift of wind.

"That's McGrath's horse," said Maurice Finn. "And that is the man gives me more trouble than anny's in this country."

Then Cleran bade him stay where he was, and riding on alone, he met McGrath.

The man laid down his load of rushes. And when he had placed his elbows on the cart, he looked at Cleran.

"It's bad weather," said he.

"It is indeed," said Cleran. "They are saying that there will be thunder before long."

"That is so," said the man. "A day to

be so sluggish as this day, there is no good thing will come out of it."

At that his wife came from the bog, stooping with her load of rushes. In her wake was a neighbour, an honest man who would say the thing that was in his mind.

Cleran spoke to these three.

"Tell me," he said, "why you would do ill to Maurice Finn from beyond the Gap?"

The woman came to where he was. And laying her hand upon his arm, she addressed him in a honeyed voice.

"Didn't you hear them saying how that is no good man at all?"

She whispered at his ear: "He put a fever on Tom Byrne, and a melancholy sickness on his wife, till there was not a hair of her head but it fell out on her."

"Listen now," said McGrath. "The best thing you could do is to tell it to the people, how if he had a brace of heifers at the fair, they shouldn't notice them. Or if he'd ask the loan of a spade, maybe, or a fistful of meal when the floods are at the ford, they'd like to let on it was promised to another. For isn't it that'll learn him?"

"Let you do that," said the woman in her honeyed voice. "For it were a pity the people to be saying you were grown too easy in your ways."

"I will tell you a tale," said Cleran. "There was a tinker who became possessed of a bad horse. And he said: 'I will beat him. It is good for him that he should be beaten.' So he beat the horse until it died."

The three leaned forward beside the cart to hear what might come next.

"That is all the tale," said Cleran.

The honest man regarded him with pity. "There was a time," said he, "you had better tales than that."

"Now there's not a thing that I told you," said McGrath, "or a word came out of my mouth, but I said it only for his good."

"Do you love him then?" asked Cleran.

"'Deed then, and we do not," said the honest man. "But if you wouldn't like a man, isn't it only a natural thing, so it is, to be at him for his good?"

Cleran smiled, shaking his head.

"My children," he said, "have I not told you that nothing is achieved by hate. For what should spring from the ashes of that flame, but weeds only?   It is a better thing to love."

There was a little pause.   But because he looked into his own mind, he did not perceive their curious glance.

"Love will make captive the weak," he said, "and bring down the strong man. Those whom men have thought most evil shall yet be redeemed of a great love."

There was another little pause.   In that far glen the stream shouted and was quiet. Then he looked up, and saw how they glanced at one another.

"Indeed your worship," said McGrath, "is it to Glendalough you're going this night? For wouldn't it be a fearful thing, the thunder of the night to come upon you, a place where no creature would be stirring?"

At this the Saint's knees seemed strange beneath him.

"You will not," said he, "because I ask you, be gentler from this out to Maurice Finn?"

"Do you see now?" said the woman. "Isn't there a deal you said, we'd like to hear it?   And aren't we saying ever and always how you were a plain man, and a kind man, and many a good turn you did us, may God help you. . . ."

"But it's how she's telling you," said the honest man; "you'll handle no pitch but 'twill stick on to you."

Meleanthus turned his head and looked at Cleran.

"That is right," said Cleran. "It is better now that we should go.   For of what avail a Saint of Heaven without authority?"

And under their cold stare, Meleanthus set out without haste, as if indeed his master left of his own choice, and had no thought of a retreat.

As for Cleran, he had forgotten Maurice Finn, who waited for him below upon the road.   For in his mind there was but the one thought—the glance of his people in that little pause.

He continued up the lonely Gap.   The heather grew scarce upon the hill.   There was nothing to be seen but a sheep here and there, that tugged at the poor grass.

Presently he heard a blatant laugh, and perceived three women who drew near to his road by a rough track of stones.   They had linked arms, and their voices rattled and shrieked in the dead air. Two of them were but young girls, but the third he knew to be the widow of Glen. Her wild hair strayed upon worn cheeks. She was not of the high lineage of the hills, possessing neither its quiet, nor listless purity of heart; for her man had brought her long since from a town beside the sea.

As their roads joined, she called to Cleran.

"Come on, lad," said she, "and we'll travel this span of road together, for they say you're a gamey man has an eye for pleasant company."

Cleran regarded her wretchedly.

"Will none leave me to my grief," he thought.

They turned into the road and began to walk at his side with swinging gait.

"Now you're the sort of man I like," said the woman. "For you're a quiet man, and a harmless man, and you've nice friendly eyes."

"I am nothing," said Cleran. And sunk in his own troubled thoughts, he rode with eyes upon the ground.

"Do you know now," said the woman, "if I seen you in a populous place, I'd say:

'That's one had the girls destroyed wherever he went by.' "

At this the girls began to laugh.

"Don't you like him better now," said they, "than Thomas Moriarty?"

"Arrah him," cried the woman. "Haven't I done with that one from this out?" And she began to sing:

"There was a hin in Ballybrent,
  She cocked her tail and away she went,
  Her lordly mate he scratched his pate . . .

"But this is a darling man has tripped my fancy altogether.

"Listen, lad," she said to Cleran. "Would you help a nice woman when she asks you? For there's a lad above that I don't like, and he's owing me these twelve days for a speckled goat."

"Of what avail," said Cleran, "to add my sorrow to your sorrow?"

The woman shot him an ill glance. "Sorrow, is it?" said she. "What's that you're saying?"

"I am sad," said Cleran. "But your despair is greater than mine."

She tossed her head. "Don't you know a lot?" said she.   And she laughed noisily.

Suddenly, her eyes were narrowed to thin slits.

"Look at him, now," began the girls.

Beneath a hag of turf, a man sat smoking leisurely. He had a crooked mouth. But he had also two beautiful brown eyes, in which a man might see nothing, because there *was* nothing, and a woman a great deal, because to her mind beauty is a mirror that must reflect its loveliest imaginings.

He took his pipe out of his mouth, and laid it carefully among the heather. "You're very welcome," said he.

"I'm after my debts," said the woman. And she met his eyes.

The man stared at Cleran.

"Mind your manners, now!" cried she. "Don't you see I'm out with a nice lad?"

"What did you do," he asked, "with Pat Daly that was digging your little field for you, and that you said would marry you at the close of winter? Did he evade you in the latter end?"

She had caught her thumb in her left hand and was twisting it to and fro in sudden jerks. "You'd know a lot!" said she.

The man turned to Cleran. "That's good company you're in," he said.

"There is no company," said Cleran, "which is not good. For whatever hides it, the jewel of perfection is in each heart."

At this the girls began to laugh.

"You owe her a debt," said Cleran. "Why is it not paid?"

"Now one might say," said the man—and he looked the Saint carefully up and down—"you to be greatly concerned along o' that one."

"Is this the first time," said Cleran sadly, "that I have meted judgement among the people?"

"Now will you tell me a reason," said the man—and he continued his careful scrutiny—"for why I would be nice to her?"

"Because she is desolate," answered Cleran. "And because she has held many in her hand, yet has been loved of none."

"Do you hear that?" said Thomas Moriarty to the woman—and at his glance, her cheeks were as burning heavy poppies in the ruin of her face. "Now about this little matter of the debt," he said to Cleran. "What would yourself be thinking should I give her for that go-at?"

"The price was settled at the fairs," said Cleran.

"Is it the price of *that* go-at! And she that grew seeking for grass 'mid the docks in the thatch of the roof! For I'm telling you, that woman's a close one."

While he talked with Cleran, he had been regarding her with a strange sideways look. Sometimes she raised her eyes, and then these encountering eyes each asked a question to which the answer was uncertain. And the question had nothing to do with the thing of which they spoke.

Suddenly he shot at the Saint an angry glance. He turned to her. "I don't like that man," he said. And picking up his pipe, he rose from the heather without haste. "Listen now," said he, "I've a job of work down at Blackditches, and if it's home you're going, we could maybe figure our debts upon the road."

"What's that you're saying?" she whispered.

"It may be, you'd be liefer stopping with himself."

With a husky laugh she ran to him. "I'll not stop with him," said she. "For don't I know it, that you're the glory of the East and West? And I like you better than they all."

She had his hands in hers.

"The devil choke you," said he. "Aren't you the ruin of all men till the end of time!"

"Isn't she the jewel of perfection!" cried the girls. And they rocked with laughter.

At that she remembered Cleran.

"Go along, and good luck to you," she mocked. "For aren't I real thankful, you to have aided a poor pitiful woman that was loved of none!"

"Hurry now," grumbled the man, "for there will be thunder before long."

"Go pity your own fancy gerrl," cried she. "But take care will you meet one now and then does have her fill of pride and splendour, and the men that are tearing one another to walk at her side upon the road."

And with linked arms they turned back into the glens, where their laughter echoed and was lost.

Cleran went upon his way.   The voice of the woman rang in his ears, till he could have imagined that it followed him.   He stopped. Her voice ceased with his footsteps, leaving a silence so ominous that he hurried on again.

But before long he had forgotten her. For his mind returned only to one thought —the glance that had passed between his people in the space of that little pause.

VII

THUNDER

THE thunder beat like a drum upon the brain.

In a roofless hut upon the hill-side, Cleran lay, staring up into the dark. Between each lightning flash the night lay heavy on his eyes. Then a square, burning and luminous, would print itself upon them, where space looked down between four walls. It had not rained as yet. The rain would bring relief.

The storm was in his brain and in his blood. Near, yet steep below him, came eddying in sharp waves a tumult of voices and of anger from beside the farm of Maurice Finn. He knew that his place was in the tumult, and yet he could not go. His shrinking mind turned in upon itself, and found there no power but a void through which he sank, clutching at derision. He saw only that brazen square, pitilessly recurring; waited but for the return of darkness, velvet cool upon his eyes.

At each illumination a slip of paper fluttered upon the ground. He knew what it contained. Yet he ignored its summons, keeping the words at a distance from his mind.

"Honoured and Holy Man,—

"Come to me here to-night for the people are gone mad after me there is John McGrath is in it and James O'Donnell and the woman of Glen does be at me like a yapping fox. It is not I that have done witchcraft or broken the laws of God.

"MAURICE FINN."

The thunder broke in the valley and was thrown to the valley beyond. You could hear it from yet three valleys more, as it returned in ever-fainting echoes.

"I cannot go," he said. "For I would but add to their confusion the tumult of my own mind, and so the clamour would be increased."

The thunder crackled above his head, and earth shook at the roar of its chariot wheels.

"I cannot go," he said. "For to-day there is no light within me, and my weakness must go down before them as a reed before a flood."

The thunder ceased. Some one passed by calling his name—an impudent voice in the night's pause.

Then Cleran rose to his feet and prayed. He called about him the three calms. The calm of the open sky; the calm of twilight fading into dusk; the calm of the un-numbered, marching stars. And at that there was laughter in his heart, and he went gladly to the door of the hut.

Now once more the world was lit. There stood around him the waiting company of the hills. While from the still farm below came a dark tumult, and a number of white faces tossed one against the other, as the leaves that a storm upturns towards the sky. They drew near, mounting the hill. But when he stood in the doorway they fell back for a moment, for his face was alight and beautiful with peace.

And he said: "What calamity has befallen

you, my people?   Have your children been struck dead?   Or are your farms swept from off the earth?   For I see that your hearts are full of trouble.''

At that the lull was broken, and many voices shouted at him together.   "It is Maurice Finn would destroy us.   Bring him up! The dirty villain! The blackguard!" While above all came the voice of the widow of Glen: "Wait now, till the sainted man will judge him.   For isn't he a great man, and an equal man, wouldn't let the one little fancy that he had be turning him from the truth of Heaven?"

Cleran lifted up his hand.   "Let McGrath speak for the rest.   For you bring me but clamour and noise.''

"Indeed," said McGrath—and his voice was as the voice of a prophet—"it is no little thing, there to be a sorcerer among us, and an eye of evil, and a destroyer.

"One little cow I had, was nicer than the rest.   White feet that were on her, a pleasant call from her mouth in the dew of morning, and she that would range the hills, taking her fill. . . .''

"Tell me what he has done," said Cleran.

"I'm telling you. Didn't he look at her this night, and the lightning that was above head? And it's how it was, that she let out a bawl. Then she give a little frisk, and away with her leaping to the Great Bog; and there was she staring and gaping the while she sank in on me till the close of time."

Cleran answered after a short while. "Now that's a strange thing, John McGrath. For don't you remember how but three years since, Maurice Finn's own cow was lost in the Great Bog, when the cloud burst over Glenamahl? It's a strange thing, he to have sent his own cow to its death."

McGrath stood, nodding his head.

"Wasn't it God Almighty did that deed, and the man owned her was a crying shame to the Christian world?"

Cleran regarded him closely. "How would you tell, John McGrath, if a beast is destroyed by God's will or by the devil? Is it that the one will go quietly, and the other will range and gambol?"

The white light trembled in the sky. And a number of flat faces were revealed, gaping foolishly at one another.

"It is my cow got a spell upon her," said

McGrath, and his face sank into the night. "You would know that," his voice continued, "on account of her eye and of her gait."

One cried from the crowd: "Was it by reason of the frisk she gave?" Out of the frayed silence—tautly and perilously suspended—there broke a thin titter that might have been laughter.

"Listen to that, mountainy men," said McGrath's unsteady voice. "He will have the plain people to laff. . . ."

The widow of Glen was at his side.

"Don't we know well," she mocked, "the Sainted man to have a fine knowledge of spells, and of the makers of spells, will bring them about him as God's candle will bring the crying dead?"

"That's it," cried McGrath. "Is it well, he to make mock of me, and another will mock him day and night?"

"May God spare him," crooned the woman, "and that one, they say, is lovelier than the moon."

At this a little murmur rose beneath him. The thunder gathered in the valley. "We heard that." "Faith, he's no proper man to be where he is!" "It's how she's saying, we should be shut of him!"

The voice of the woman lashed the storm. "The poor man," she moaned, rocking to and fro with delight. "The fine darlin' man was better than the rest. What is he now? . . ."

"What is he indeed?" they said. "Let him go away out of this, or he'll not like it!"

Then Cleran prayed once more. And his prayer was that the lightning should come quickly, for in the darkness he was alone and without power.

As the breath of the people touched him, the lightning came. The faces were no longer flat and white. They were close against his face. He saw the smoke in-grained upon them and how they were damp in the sullen heat. He saw how one man had a wall eye.

And he stood still, and spoke very gently. "I have healed your little sick children. I am homeless and without wealth because of you. Do not that which you will weep for in the morning, for I have loved you without measure."

They did not answer.

"Look at now!" cried the woman, and she began to laugh immoderately. "They will grow tame and lick his hand like little cats!"

But her voice faded with the lightning, for the rest were turning sadly away.

The sky softened and great drops fell from it like tears.

And Cleran thought: "Where is Maurice Finn? He is not here at my side. In the tumult he has slunk away to hide his head." For in his heart there was no joy, only a great weariness with himself, and with his people, and with all that he had ever said or done.

He heard Meleanthus neigh under the wall. And he thought: "Some wayfarer is approaching." But he did not turn.

The sky let fall its burden of rain.

And now he knew that it was no longer dark, but that in each rain-drop the light of the hidden dawn was caught like a snared bird.

Then a hand touched his hand. And looking down, he saw that Keth stood beside him. Her hair was smooth and wet, her face a little paler than the night.

THUNDER

"The storm is over," she said.   "The sun will rise on the wet leaves, and on the budding tender beech leaves, in a valley that is far from here.   And there is rest in that for the sick heart.

"Labour is vain," she said, "and there is no such thing as a reward.   But there is love.   And that is cool and radiant, and in it are enclosed all quiet things.

"Come away," she said.   "For you have waited too long in a parched dream."

Then he saw but one way before him.

For in the beginning he had said: "She is a home."   And next he had said: "She is pity."   But now he knew that he wanted nothing in the world but to follow whither she would go.

She closed her two hands upon his hand, and brought him where the horse waited.

VIII

THEY BEGIN THEIR TRAVELS

When Cleran and Keth went out from the hills they travelled by many and strange roads.

They went southward first to lonely Allen, and to Abbeyleix of the dark soil, where the streams make no sound. From here, they joined the clamorous high-road. All envied him as they passed: at dusk the children ceased their play, and whispered together that a queen went by, while in the red-throated forge men raised their clinking tools and paused to watch them out of sight. They reached Waterford of the golden furze; then turning to the west, came to wild Kerry, where by the sea the little farms are as white flowers, and the voice of the people is gentle as a summer wave.

And wherever they went, men welcomed

them because of her great beauty; since
though there was some talk among the plain
folk, she was not known to their masters,
and the rumour had not yet reached them
that she was a fairy or perhaps a witch.   As
time passed there were still some gold coins
in the Saint's wallet.   His little store was
scarcely touched.   For everywhere the men
came running to their wives, bidding them
cook their rarest dishes.   And—did these
shrewder ones shake their heads, and whisper that beauty was but an ill pledge—they
declared that all women were ill-natured,
that there was beauty *and* beauty, and that
they knew a good woman when they saw
one.

At Cleran they glanced inquiringly.   But
he avoided those eyes, because at their question he must have looked back and searched
his heart.   And at that time he cared only to
think of the immediate hour.

As for Keth, she accepted what they
offered.   For she thought: "When my lover
is alone with me he does not look at me
overmuch, for he says, 'She is there beside
me.   In the shadow her long glance awaits
me.   And I am well content.'   But when

I speak with other men his face is drawn and pale, and his dazed eyeballs stare before him blindly as if the world fell from his feet. And that pleases me."

So she played upon men's hearts, and as on a slender instrument of strings, troubled what chord she would. Where she had passed, their eyes were empty. They found no more splendour in the sun, or in the dew, or in games of hurling and of skill.

Yet to her, this ruin brought no equal joy.

Should Cleran reprove her, she did but sigh wearily and shake her head.

"Do not chide me," she said. "For indeed I cannot taste the apple, but only the sharp quince. And in all the world there is nothing new."

Day by day she would hurry onward, as if always over the next hill had been the goal she sought. At daybreak she was impatient to be gone. The night came all too slow to hide the out-worn day. If in the twilight Cleran would have paused, and from the dark earth surveyed the untroubled West, she would pluck his sleeve and bid him hasten, for: "It is too sad," she said, or: "I have seen it so often." And all at once she would be very gay. "When it is dark," she'd say, "let us fish for trout in the hill streams, for that will make us glad again." Or: "Let us go where there is joy and dancing." And they would hasten to the next town.

On a warm night, they fished beside a Kerry stream. They had climbed till the dusk grew soft upon their eyes; then she had lit a lantern, and held it over a dark pool. The dim trout rose up without sound and, with their foolish gaping mouths, came straining to the light. Now and again she struck her line and drew in a fish; from between her fingers its leaping heart went out, and was gone she knew not where.

Cleran watched her. The lamp lit her cold face, and the point where, in a rippled circle, her line touched the stream. "Do you know," she said, "a man is never so happy as when he is killing some thing? For to be happy is to be more skilful than your neighbours. And there is no such test of skill." The night grew chill. And he thought: "She is cold as death."

But presently she turned back; and wondering, he perceived that her eyes were miserable.   For a moment that was a year, each existed but in the deep places of the other's eyes.   "Do not forsake," she said.

Then, with a light laugh, she rose.

He collected the sticky trout, where they grew stiff among the grass, and returned beside her eagerly.

So they travelled till spring grew old.

As they came into Clare the bramble flowered, in the hedges the wild-rose hung listless, and dust whitened the parched leaves.   Their steps flagged in the heat. His love, growing day by day, was the more powerless to make her glad.

But one morning there came from behind them a messenger, who led a quivering slender horse.   "I am to bring him to you from my master," said he.   "And if you should come back this way, I am to say you must dine with him again, and a thousand welcomes that will be before you." He gazed bitterly at the black horse.   "He's a damn good one," shouted he; "and the best we had, may the Lord help us!"   And at that he fled for his life the way he'd come, having no doubt that did he look again, he'd be turned into a frog for his ill-manners,

THEY BEGIN THEIR TRAVELS

As for Keth, she was beside herself with joy. For a while the horse was her one delight, because its eyes were terrified and angry, and because it was quiet in her hands.

I X

BUTTERFLY

ONE day, she wandered alone among the fields, for it was too hot to ride. The sun had parched her throat, her limbs grew heavy in the heat. Presently the grass deepened about her ankles, and there mounted coolly to her ears the gurgle of a brook. She went near and found, hidden among the yellow flags, a little boat tied to a plank.

"O, I am weary with the hot earth," she said. And loosing the boat, she paddled out from among the reeds and began to drift idly down-stream.

At first her brook flowed with shallow talk among the fields. Absorbed in its own chatter, it curled on the sleek green backs of stones. An hour went by, and it grew wider. A bridge of one arch spanned its breadth; in reaches gilded and luminous, the waving trout lay with heads upstream or darted from before her bows.

Keth remembered that Cleran would perhaps be missing her. But because she was in an idle mood, she did not trouble to turn back.

The banks withdrew to either hand. Shimmering outspread, her stream rustled by wide shallows. A bridge of two arches spanned its breadth where, haunch-deep in the dark water, the cows stood and flicked with their tails the droning flies. They considered her with staring eyeballs, till laughing, she caught a black cow by the horn. In that flickering gloom their panic boomed about her, beating with hollow shout against the piers. She left its babel behind her and sailed out into the sunlight.

Her river deepened. It came into the level marshes: of a sudden it grew secret, flowing silent and sleek as oil. As afternoon drew on a small wind fluttered on its face, so that the round lily-leaves stood up from the water as if they would have looked at her, then dropped to the surface with a little slap. She wondered if Cleran had gone out to seek her. But the little wind fluttered so coolly that she did not trouble to turn back. For, "To be happy," she said, "is a rare thing. But to be unhappy is common as the light, so that it is better to make the most of joy than to shield another from distress."

A swan came by, followed in single file by his meek family. He puffed out his beautiful feathers, and with red bill sunk in his soft breast, came at her in the splendour of rage. When he had come as near as seemed to him discreet, he returned to make ready for another charge; and this brave show he repeated many times while his family applauded from hoarse throats. His wife's feathers were as fine as his: but being a creature of discretion, she did not make a show of this, but laid them flat upon her sides that they might seem of an inferior mould. Presently her children grew weary of their father, and turned to fish for weeds on the river bottom, so that their great bodies waved in the air like flags. But with slim neck and modest wing, their mother stayed dutifully, and watched the prowess of her husband.

Evening arrived. Trout rose beneath

the yellow sky: the widening river grew so quiet that it did not seem to move at all. Presently a road drew near, bringing the unlovely houses. A bridge of three arches spanned the stream, where the young men had gathered after their day's work. The children shouted to either hand. Yet their clamour did but contrive to make that yellow reach seem quieter.

At length she came to a great house, which stood close beside the river in the midst of a garden of such beauty as her imagination had not dreamed. At this she drew in to land and, making fast the boat, set out through the garden. She flitted hither and thither, touching a flower here and a leaf there, smelling the rose-buds that stooped across her path. There were lawns soft as velvet with edges cut sharp as gingerbread. There were a hundred trees carved to gigantic shapes, and ten borders containing only the rarest flowers. Yet the blinds of the house were drawn. And in all this loveliness no voice rang, and no step was heard upon the gravel.

Keth drew near the house. And suddenly, in the yard beside it, she came upon a little stable-boy clanking his boots and whistling merrily.

When he perceived her he stopped. "O my Lars!" he said. And putting his thumb in his mouth, he stared at her in amazed delight.

"Tell me," said Keth, "who lives in this house."

"They're the lords of Cong," answered he. "They have great riches."

"Perhaps," said Keth, "they will give me lodging for the night."

The little stable-boy looked at the ground. "There's room enough," said he.

Then Keth went to the door and rang.

Presently a shuffling of feet was heard within, and an old retainer thrust out his head.

"What is it you are wanting?" he said.

"I lost my way," answered Keth. "I would see your masters and ask a lodging for the night."

The old man grinned at her with malice. "And what message will I give," he asked, "that will bring them to see you?"

"Tell them I am beautiful," answered she.

At that he left her upon the doorstep.

But presently he returned, bowing pro-fusely. "The lords of Cong will speak with you," he said. And he led her through ten long galleries where each carpet was deeper than the last, each vase and hanging of a rarer craftsmanship. But it was hard to see them well. For the blinds were drawn lest the sun fade them.

In the heart of these, they came upon a little room where the air was of a stifling closeness. It was illumined by two flares that stood in their own grease on a battered table, and breathed into the air a bitter smoke. The light of day might not reach it. For there was no window.

Two blind men sat at the table. With nervous fingers, they were counting gold coins into hundreds and piling them one upon the other. When they had counted a thousand, they called in a messenger and sent him to some far land, bidding him find what never yet was bought and bring it to them there.

They blinked at Keth with their blind eyes.

"Are you considered to be beautiful?"

said one. "Then you do well to be where you are, for there is nothing in this house but is of the most rare perfection."

"There is the most intricate ceiling in the world," said the other, "and the picture from Egypt which ten seers could not understand. There is a horse in the stable which could go round the world while the rest were racing round a hill."

"Indeed," whined the old retainer, "you'd not wonder! For who is it has the taste of the lords of Cong?"

"The value of beauty," said the first, "is that many would possess it. But it begins to grow too common. A few years more," he said, "and I will begin to make a feature of ugliness. For by then its rarity should command a price."

"But would not that offend your taste?" fawned the old servant.

"I have never seen beauty," answered he. "I shall not see ugliness either."

"As to this lady," said his servant, and he bowed once more, "what is it your wish that I should do for her?"

"Since she is beautiful, you had best bid her stay," he answered. "But do not trouble us with her company. For we have work to do."

And stooping, they began once more to drop the clinking coins, and to pile them into little heaps.

Then the old man led her by passages and stairs, until they came to a great room where the walls were of a clouded amber, the bed-posts, twisting trees of jade. And when he had put a tray of delicacies before her, he left her to her own company.

Keth's delight knew no bounds. Out-side it had begun to rain, and the noise of it made yet more radiant her bright room. She moved here and there, touching the silken hangings where proud beasts lurked and curled azaleas bloomed; crouching among the bedclothes with the lamp held high above her head, till among those intricate branches, a thousand jewels flashed like singing birds. The lamp was a cup hewn from a single sapphire; not a mirror upon the walls, but it winked from the heart of some rare jewel. When it grew late and she put out the light, she had gathered these treasures close about her, that she might see them as soon as she awoke. With a

H

sweet sound, the raindrops fluttered the leaves beyond the window. She nestled in her soft bed, and fell asleep.

When she awoke next day, the sunlight gleamed on the wet leaves. She sprang from her bed with a childish joy, and taking a mirror from the table, began to flash it in the sun; for wherever it flashed, there shone a little arc of green or pink or orange light. As for her poor lover, she did not think of him overmuch, for she said: "It may be he is sad without me. And if I too grow sad, I make his grief of no avail, for to neither of us has it brought delight."

Presently she went down. As she passed by that inner room, she saw that the flares were lit already: while with heads bent close, the two blind men sat, counting their gold.

"There is nothing," whispered one, "that will so increase the splendour of a house, as a fair mistress."

"Yet she must be kept from the great rooms," said the other, "for fear she would break something of value."

"She will grow quiet soon enough," said the first. "It may be," he whispered, "she also has riches."

BUTTERFLY

Outside, the old retainer crept near with a stealthy tread. For the last messenger had let fall three gold coins that twinkled from the carpet.

Keth passed by, and went out from them into the yard, where in the glancing sunlight the stable-boy groomed a brown filly.

He sang as he worked:

> "The little sweet lark is in the meadows,
> The little sweet lark is in the sky.
> I will go wandering, wandering,
> Till I will fold between my hands the
> downy fluttering sweet lark"

while now and again he threw his arms about her, and kissed her on her two ears and on her mane.

But when he saw Keth he ceased his work, and blushed crimson to the temples.

Then Keth called him, bidding him come and play with her in the garden and show her where the fruit was ripest. Together they raced upon the lawns, burying their faces in the hydrangeas ponderous with raindrops, chasing the white butterflies, that hung each as an ultimate petal on the larkspur flowers.

But as time passed she remembered Cleran.

"I must be going now," she said; and seeing how his round foolish mouth fell open, she stooped down and kissed him on the forehead.

"That's for the brown filly," she told him. And she left the garden, and set off without haste to seek her lover.

It happened that before long she came across him, for he had travelled far in search of her. His eyes were staring and empty in his haggard face. The rain, which had fluttered the leaves beyond her window, had soaked all night into his coat, so that by morning it was stiff and cold.

She stole up to him, guilty and smiling.

"What has befallen you?" he said. "I thought you had been drowned in the black pond where the alders are."

At that she grew sullen. For she was in a merry mood, and his dismal looks made her unhappy—as it were a blot on the fabric of her joy.

"My heart has been light," she said. "Do you not see? The sun is shining."

He gazed at her forlornly. "Must you,"

she cried, "so fill the day with gloom? I would I had stayed where I was."

They turned, and set out with sad steps. The sun shone guiltily on the winking leaves as if it should not have been there.

"I suppose," he said, "that one day you will leave me and not come back."

She dropped her eyes and, to his outraged thought, appeared to smile. Then her lashes were drawn up, and the full blaze of her beauty laughed upon him. "O terrible one!" she mocked. "O cloud of thunder!"

In his despair, he held her in his arms. "Do you not love me?" he begged. "Say only that you love me!"

But she was angry, because from this out her day was full of gloom.

X

THE SAINT GROWS VERY SICK

AFTER this, did she so much as leave him for a moment, he was beside himself with fear. Not one who crossed their path, but he divined in him a hidden purpose to steal her from his side. To his troubled mind her face was eloquent of that which least was near her heart. In her voice, when she addressed a stranger, there was a perilous sweetness; her wandering glance would hold him spell-bound, while in that quietness fury and impotence mocked one another.

He grew silent in her company. Let him but look upon her and the words were frozen at his lips. At that she would chide him merrily because he was so poor a lover, yet in her laughter there was the bite of scorn. "My poet," she would say, and,

"My juggler in swift words!   Is it not good to be beside you?"

He regarded her, helpless.

"I am ill-versed," he pleaded, "in the small ways of the craft of love. But you must teach me what you can."

As time passed the pride went from his step.   His glance grew ill at ease and might not rest.   Did he encounter the people of those parts as they cleared the bushes of a ditch, or, it might be, drove to the fair behind a ragged mountainy horse, he did not look at them.   For it seemed to him that they regarded him with a kind of pity, or that they laughed to see him thus undone.

So intent was his mind upon one theme, that before long all else seemed weariness. The tin vessels in his pack—which must serve their solitary meals—grew rusted and stained with grease.   His coat was shabby and ill-cared. There was a rent in his sleeve which still he left undarned.   It came about that each day they set out a little later than the last: for by the fall of night, they must obtain to no place in particular; while, resting at her side in some cool brake or little field where the hay was sweet, he was reluctant to bring her again into the perilous world. And when at length they came to the day's end, he was so impatient for her company that he would leave his horse uncared. For an hour, perhaps, Meleanthus wandered in the grass with the pack fallen askew upon his back, and the rein trailing till he trod upon it, and hurt his tender mouth.

So they travelled still to the Westward, by the little hills and by the unnumbered crooked roads which brought them to the sea. And, whether it were on the parched roads or on the cliffs where sea-gulls made their cry, he thought of her only. Yet seeing him so she grew impatient: because her heart, being sad, would have rested in his care, yet looking to him for sanctuary, found but the ruin that herself had wrought.

X I

SHE IS ANGRY

THE day was hot and she was angry. She did not know with whom she was angry. It might have been herself.

This morning she had hurt her lover. "I shall ride to Cruachan to-day," she said. "But do not come with me. For I am weary of your company." And as she said this, she was filled at once with such pity for him, and such fury, that she could well have wept.

Cleran was carving a stick from a root of larch. He did not look at her, but continued with a scrupulous care to shave the mealy wood. From his dark knife the parings crimped and fell.

"It is as you will," he said. "When you are gone, there are many things that I would do." And dropping his knife, he began to polish the soft wood where the blade left its print.

She came and stood beside him.

"Maybe," she said, "when I come back to-night, you will still be rubbing at that branch. You will have polished it till there is nothing left but a gleam in the dark between your hands."

Cleran did not answer.

"Your hand is trembling," she said. "It is a pity, the hand of a strong man to tremble."

He looked at her, and his face was still. "If you are riding to Cruachan," he said, "you had better go quickly. It is a long road." And for a moment they stared at one another with miserable eyes.

Then she went to put bridle on the horse.

The horse saw her come and turned his heel to her, with ears strained back and flickering glance. Keth sprang past him. She jerked the bit into his teeth: they struggled together, while, between the straps of the bridle, she crushed his twitching ears. As she tightened the saddle-girths he arched his neck, and snapped at the bit with a grinding noise. She caught his soft upper lip and held him so, while she laughed to see his impotent rage.

Then she came back to Cleran. The sting was gone out of her anger. "I am going now," she said: and with a rueful smile she waited, watching him.

Now because of the struggle she panted, while upon her cheeks bloomed a soft blush. And seeing her, he was filled with a misery so helpless that his heart cried out for solitude, so that alone he might endure this pain. "It is as you will," he said.

Her eyes grew cold.

"There was a time," she said, "when you were taller by a head than I. Why have you grown so bowed?"

And seeing him wince, she thrust the deeper. "If you should go back into the hills," she said "they would not know you. They would say: 'He was no plain man that left us, but a prince high and proud.'"

And at that she went from him in a cold blaze of anger, because he had not chid her, but stared at her only with miserable eyes.

Out upon the roads the horse would not fight her. He chose to simulate exhaustion; her heels raised no stir in his limp body, in the heat of noon he grew heavy as earth. Had he but fought her she would have been glad.

She entered a town to ask a drink of water. The streets were filled with buying and selling, with dust and sleepy cur-dogs. The monotonous stir of cartwheels, of footsteps and of voices played upon the nerves.

Many carts were drawn across the road. Their owners had forgotten them, for they were talking pleasantly to one another. There was no reason that men should be light-hearted in so squalid a street.

A jennet and a flat cart out of the country blocked her way, till pausing with impatient fingers, she called out to know who was its master. "Do you know where is Philly gone?" an urchin called to his comrade across the road. "I couldn't tell," replied the other. "It might be he is in at Hennessy's, or it might be he is below in the Square, or it might be he is in at Doolan's up the street." Three or four collected as flies about jam to debate on the matter of the cart. "Will we dhraw him from the road ourself?" said one. "Give him a puck

and he'll stir so," said the next.   He dragged
at the rein.   The jennet thrust his four feet
into the ground, while his body swayed with
a backward motion.   "He'll not move," said
the boy, and he grinned broadly.   His friend
considered the creature with a solemn air.
"He must be terrible fond of Philly," said he.

Because she could have laughed her rage
increased.   The jennet stood with chin
thrust out.   That it regarded her with a
mild eye, but chafed her wretched anger.
She turned to find another way.

A woman with a black shawl, and eyes that
hooded like an eagle's in sudden flashes,
told a dramatic story to her neighbour.
" And I said: 'May God spare ye, Mrs.
O'Mahony, and may he take my own soul
that is in me, and dhrag it crying through
the galleries of hell, if it was in *my* house
your jug was cracked or broken.'"   Her
barrow of streaked mackerel glinted out in
the road.   In the dust beside her neighbour's
boots were a bundle of pigs' trotters.

Keth saw that a butcher, in his white
apron, would have given her a drink for the
simple pleasure of speaking with her; and
determined not to ask him.   A greyhound

came from the butcher's shop, and on its head were two drops of red blood.

The barrow was in her path. She drove the horse at the narrow space beside it, but he hung back, shuddering; while the woman thought only of her tale. She struck him and he stood up. The people crushed back from where he was. Then his terror gave way beneath her heel, and he danced by. Yet his knee touched the axle, and it seemed that half the street came down in echoing crashes. Like a thin shower of silver, the mackerel slipped pattering to the road.

She did not stay to hear the murmurs of the people. The horse—his knee still smarting—came to life and trembled in her hands. Before long they left the town behind them.

Now his mood matched with her own. His tingling coat was quick as fire, his resentment was joined with hers in equal fight. The pressure of her hand to right or left caused him to pull out in the reverse direction. Did she press him on with too great urgency, he stopped stark in the middle of the road and, sidling into the ditch, reared and kicked out savagely. She nursed his wrath. His anger fed the fire of hers;

from out these intertwining flames grew a splendour that was near delight. While with her right hand and with her heels she urged him forward, her left that held the reins would foster his revolt. But of a sudden she forced him from his stand, and gathering speed, they fled for two miles or three on the uneven grass at the road's edge, till both were so weary they could go no farther. At that they came to a pause upon some little rise of ground, and with the reins flung loose upon his neck he stood lifeless for a full five minutes, while she lolled, her shoulder upon his quarters. The lust of her anger was appeased. Presently he turned back his head, surprised at her quietness; and she, perceiving how the white blaze ran down his nose and turned to a babyish pink when it halved his distended nostril, indolently stroked that velvet lip. She spoke to him too with teasing words that were now tender, now full of torment; while he cocked his ears back and forth, divided between nervousness and inquiry.

After a while they continued on their way. But as time passed she grew tired of riding, and dismounting, lashed him carelessly to a tree as was her wont, and continued upon foot. When she had gone a little distance she heard a struggle behind her, and observed that she had tied him so close that he could not move his head, or reach the patch of green grass which lay temptingly beneath. In a sudden whim she left him so, with white eyes and body strained taut against the curb. But all through the evening he haunted her, sometimes as a sadness, sometimes as a bitter satisfaction, sometimes as a pity beyond endurance.

XII

THEIR HEARTS CHANGE

WHEN time passed and Keth did not return, Cleran was beside himself with fear. To his distraught imagination unnumbered terrors came and chased one another to and fro, until it seemed that the fabric of his mind must break. But as day waned, for a moment his despair fell from him. And grown weary with too much distress, he turned his face towards the sea.

As he drew near to the cliffs, a little wind blew from the salt waves and ruffled the hair upon his brow. And he began to reason with himself; "To what a pass am I come!" he said. "For time was when no evil chance might break the quiet of my spirit: so that the sad of heart drew near and rested their care in that still place, where was room for all sorrow and all joy. But now at the whim of one I am flung this way and that. And if men would find peace, they must go far from where I am."

At this he looked up into the South, at whose pin-point centre the sky trembled, for in that hour a star was born. And suddenly he was glad, because for an hour Keth might not touch him, and he was freed from the slavery of her glance. As his heart grew still silence came near. Till listening, he heard the quiet stars singing out of sight.

Presently, from the dim strand there came to his ears the keen of grief. And looking down, he saw three women who sat beside the waves. The tide came running to their feet; while, drawing their dark shawls about their heads, they rocked to and fro.

Then Cleran went down by the cliff path and laid his hands upon them, and in gentle words asked them of their trouble.

"They are gone out," said one, "and they are not come back."

"Yesterday," said another, "they went from us, going to the North. The light was in the moon, but it was not in the stars yet. Now the stars are come again. But they are not come."

While she spoke, a little child ran to her across the pebbles and plucked her shawl.

"Will you listen, mother," it said, "till I tell you of the fine ship I made. It is the grandest ship in all the ring o' the world."

But the mother loosed its clinging hand.

"This morning," she said, "I put cake for my man upon the fire, and tea, and the bit of meat that he would use." And she began to cry the louder. "The day is grown old to me," she said. "The grief of a mother in her pains was never longer than this day."

"Have you no boat," said Cleran, "or no man among you, that we may seek them?"

"There is a boat in the cove above," they said, "and the sails that are stretched out and drying there among the stones; but it would take three men beside yourself to draw her here athwart the strand. And aren't we alone with ourselves only?" they moaned.

At that Cleran looked behind him, and saw three men who came to him from the shore. The first was a rough man with great shoulders. The second was a small dark man. But the third was tall and shining, and his eyes were deeper than the night.

"Why did you come?" said Cleran to the first.

"I do not know," he answered. "But as I was drawing turf upon the hill a herd passed me, and he said: 'You are wanted below on the strand.' So I came down."

"And why did you come?" he asked the next.

"I do not know," he answered. "But as I was gathering in my bit of hay, a lad passed me, driving his flock out of the East. And he said: 'You are wanted below upon the strand.' So I came down."

As they turned to bring the boat, Cleran walked beside the third. "Why did you come?" he said.

"I know," answered he, "and you know also." And the Saint thought: "My wandering desire is at an end."

In a little while, they came upon a tar-black boat where she sprawled aslant upon the beach. They furled her sails from the gritting sand and ran her down the thunderous shingle, till the pebbles grew dark beside the waves. As they went their shadows became sharp, for now the moon had risen. Yet by the third stranger there was no shadow.

Then from the echoing boat his comrades brought out the rudder, and the oars with flashing blades, while the moonlight shone upon their hands. But Cleran stood beside the stranger. And about him the wind ceased. And the shadow of calm was on his heart.

He spoke beneath his breath.

"I have done ill," he said.

"The ship waits," said the stranger, "and the wind is fair."

"Is this the end?" said Cleran.

"A debt is not paid," answered he.

"I would escape," said Cleran.

"There is no escape. But where each is come, guiding his own star, there shall he yet do well or ill."

Then Cleran entered the boat; and with their frail oars, his comrades pushed her from the strand. The stranger did not come with them. But staying on the shore, he stood by the women and watched them go.

When they had gone a little distance, they rose in the plunging boat and loosed the sails. A cloud passed over the moon's face, and the wind blew fresher from the

South. The sails flapped and stiffened in the breeze. And the dark sea ran past; till gurgling, it sucked at her keel with a low song.

Cleran took the tiller. The care fell from his shoulders. He lifted up his head, and sailed joyously into the night. For the salt of the sea was in his mouth. And his heart sang.

Presently there came a little wave and furtively slapped at the boat's side. They looked up and saw beside them a dark headland, and beyond it, the unbounded churning sea.

The men grew troubled and turned to Cleran.

"Where is it we are going?" said they.

"We are going to Inischree in the North," said Cleran. "For there is no other place between here and Emlagh, where a boat might founder in a calm sea."

"We can't go there," they said. "A man to go among those rocks, he would perish surely."

"Are you afraid?" said Cleran. And he began to put the ship about. "See," he said, "we will turn back and tell these women that where we dared not go their men have perished."

"We are not afraid," murmured the men. So he brought her to the open sea.

As they cleared the Point he bore up before the wind, till trembling she rose on the wave and raced with it to the hidden North; while the stiff wind whistled in the shrouds.

A thundering rose to the North-west. Now and again, a little white tongue licked at the sky. "What is that?" asked Cleran.

"That is the Spit of Inis," said they—and they glanced uneasily at the Saint. "A man to turn upon that Spit, he'd be well roasted."

"What of three men?" cried Cleran. And laughing, he turned his ship towards Inis.

They drew near. The great rocks darkened in their path; from beneath, foam floated back upon sleek eddies. Bidding them furl the sail, Cleran called to them to bring out their oars.

Now they ran in upon the tide. From the clouds, the wayward moon flew out. They saw the many tossing waves and the rocks oil-bright or cavernous. In their midst they saw two derelict masts, where the huddled cormorants crouched, birds of the sea. . . .

They were no birds. They were men who clung to their lost ship that, spitted upon some hidden rock, swung to and fro. Anon they were flung up to heaven, anon swooped down, splashed of the laughing waves.

"We are come," said Cleran to his men.

They were running in at a great speed. The roar of thunder was about them; breakers flashed in the night, darting their spears. The wreck swung lower and, with eyes upturned, its huddled freight struck the curled waves, flinging sprays of silver to the indifferent moon. They opened their mouths. Yet no shout came from them in that noise of waters.

Then the Saint swung the tiller, and with strained sinews brought his ship about, until her stern was to the shore. "Now steady her," he called to his men. So that they bowed their backs, and against the floods of night leaned their frail oars.

Now the wreck dipped, and the smooth waves washed where it had been. It rose, and the crew came up with twisting arms: from the mast-head water fell in showers,

"Pull harder," cried Cleran, "for we must go no further."

They lay close upon the wreck to seaward. The men strained so that their craft paused, and in that wrack stood still, her timbers shuddering. The Saint rose, standing in the stern. And lifting a rope, he judged his time, and flung it toward the dipping masts.

With snatching fingers, the wreck's crew caught it one by one, and loosed their hold of the buffeting mast. As a stone drops, each sank into the sea. Then the tautening rope tugged at his hands; his dead weight was dragged up and brought gently in over the side.

When all were safe, the Saint bade his men that they pull for the open sea. Yet though the oars plunged they made no way, for the tide was strong in that place; till taking the westward oar, he cried to his comrades that both should pull the other. But at the westward oar he pulled alone, as though he had been two men.

So they came safely from beneath the rocks.

The tumult died. Cat-like and delicate,

the little waves played at the bows. And falling at their feet, the men called down blessings on these three, who had brought them from so great a peril.

So when the sail was set they gathered way, and turned with long tacks for the homeward shore.

At daybreak—when in the colourless dawn the cold drops glisten on the oar-blades—they grounded their keel upon the strand. Here many were gathered to receive them, for it had gone about the country that a man without fear was come into those parts.

They thronged about him.

"Heaven spare him," cried the women. "He blessed himself and the sea before him. Indeed, he blessed himself, and the sea before him."

"God is good," they said, "and he with power in his hands, putting splendour on the one he loves."

With shining face he went among them. "This alone," he said, "is a wonderful thing: that in this place, as of old, the shadowy doors have been flung back. For in the night there came to us heralds whom we know not, and sent us at your need."

Then, on the margin of the crowd, he saw the white face of Keth that stared at him with hollow eyes. And in that moment he hated her, because she had taken from him all he had.

She drew closer, and touched him with her fingers. "You are not gone away," she said.

Then he saw that she shivered in the night.

And pitifully, as an anxious mother with her child, he took her hand and led her to the sleeping shore. He folded his rough coat about her and comforted her with gentle words. "Do not tremble so," he said, "for I will not leave you any more. Have I not said it long ago, that I will cherish you to the end of time?"

But Keth thought only of his face when first he saw her upon the strand.

And fear gripped her heart.

XIII

MELEANTHUS

A FINE rain descended from the hills and from the desolate bogs of Maam, and drifted across the lake.

Upon that slope of bogged grass which the men of this townland call the Fairgreen, many strange persons collected for the fair. About them a crowd already gathered; for here gaiety was scarce, and the rain so common as to be despised. There were a man and his wife who sold oranges and Peggy's Leg from a little booth. There were jugglers in cards, and even in white mice. As the light waned, the tent of a circus was going up. The huge canvas bellied and grew taut. Within a lamp shone out: dark upon light, little men struggled with the poles. And there was a woman who conducted a game of chance, whose cry was at once alluring and terrible. It leaped at the throat of one high scream, where, with a fearful tenacity, it hung suspended; then its gabbled words fell tumbling to the common murmur. "Try . . . yer luck in coppers!" "Try . . . yer luck in coppers!" Across that unaccustomed valley, it tore at the rocks and raked the little fields. At its call the young men would hazard three coppers or perhaps a sixpenny. It drew them back with their last pence from the distant corners of the green.

Cleran and Keth rode by, coming from the sea.

"Look," cried Cleran, "what a gay scene! Let us go and watch the circus play. Would it not cheer you?" And though she seemed half reluctant, they turned their horses up the field; and leaving them where a ditch gave shelter from the driving rain, were lost among the crowd.

Of the black horse there is nothing to tell in the hour which followed, since his life was enacted in no outward sphere, but within the tragic circle of his mind. Not so with Meleanthus. The tinkers' horses grazed along the ditch and, with collars fallen about their ears, exchanged after many months such taunts and pleasantries as were their delight. For him this was a great day. For he had made no public appearance since he was the horse, not of a mere tinker, but of a Saint of Heaven.

A trace-clipt pony edged towards him. Its harness smelled of grease and was full of cracks. "You had great fortune," it ventured, "since I last seen you."

"You may say that I did," said Meleanthus. "Though to be responsible for a Saint, that is no light thing."

Another shambled near. "And is he a real Saint?" asked he.

"He is of course," said Meleanthus. "Praying he has, that would knock the roof out of the sky, and the demons you'd hear scattering from him in the dead of night."

"Now! Isn't that wonderful," said a black horse with large hip-bones. He had yellow teeth and a long upper lip.

They began to press about him.

"And what like is he?" said they.

"He is a nice man," said Meleanthus, "but without sense. Indeed, there are times when he would miss his nourishment and sleep if it were not for myself.   But for all that," he said, "he is a Saint of Heaven; and you'd not see one of *them* every day."   And tucking in his tail, he backed from the rain into a hedge of briars.

"I suppose," they said, "you stop only in the best houses."

"That depends upon the neighbourhood," said Meleanthus.   "You can imagine that, where there are grand houses, they are fighting one another to have us.   And of course there is no asking a sup here and a sup there, or letting on to be what you are not."

It grew dark.   The organ of a merry-go-round struck up in the field below.   The rain fell steadily.

"On Friday," said Meleanthus, "we took supper with the Knight of Rory; and last Monday—I think it was—we stopped with his Grace of Rathcarogue."

"Well, now.   Isn't that wonderful!" murmured the horse with the long lip.

"No doubt," said a red jennet the colour of a carrot, "they kep' great state in the mansion."

"They did of course; but without vulgarity or show.   Lacqueys they had—that is the gentlemen who conduct the household—nice style, don't you know, chalk in the hair and such-like. Now in the stables there was not the same tone. . . . But indeed, I'm talking too much of what you'd not know of."

"Yet for why," said a little ass with a mouse's tail, "did you go quit from your own place?"

Meleanthus glanced at him coldly.

"At present," he said to the others, "we are doing a little trip among the plains. But we will be finished with that before long, for my master has lost his spirits since there is no one asking him advice. For indeed," he said, "we were consulted upon every matter." And growing weary of such common talk, he began to eat a thistle.

The merry-go-round played its three tunes: rhythm of four, "the Rakes of Mallow"; rhythm of three, "The Wild Hills of Clare"; merry galloping rhythm. Then it began again. Meleanthus licked his lips and thought awhile. They all waited.

"It's like this," he said. "There are plenty nice men here and there—tinkers knocking through the world, giving no trouble to any but themselves—pleasant men that will

make rhymes and songs, or go higgling fishes
with an ass and car.   Yet if I'd mention them
in my talk, a person never heard of them.

"But do you see, a Saint of Heaven, he
has class.   Now if you were to say: 'The
Lord Mayor of Cork is coming to these
parts,' or if you'd say: 'The King of France
is here,' it would be the one thing with saying,
ourselves were here."

"Well, now——" began the black horse.

"Yet my master has a great name," said
the little ass with the mouse's tail.   "He'd
blow a tin whistle and dance at the one time;
and when he'd grow tired whistling it wid his
mouth, he'd whistle it wid his no-as."

There was an awkward silence.

"That is a nice accomplishment," said
Meleanthus, "but it would not be thought
well of by the better sort of people."

He turned to the others.   "Such a commotion as there 'll be," he said, "when we
go back to our own country: crowds gathering in every place."

"I suppose," said the jennet, "one would
hold the head high and take no heed of
them."   At the idea, she tossed her golden
mane.

"No, indeed," said Meleanthus. "It is thought better of, to be friendly without familiarity. For to be common, and to be plain in your style, that is the manner of the gentry." And backing side-ways, he squeezed himself into the dyke behind him; so that with a polite finality the briars closed above his head.

"The divil mend you," said a voice.

He looked, and saw that there was another in the dyke before him. This was a pony of yellowish-white appearance, with stump ears, and a mane that had been hogged once.

"Well, now," said Meleanthus. "To think we'd meet!"

"That was fine talk," said the white pony, "you were giving them in the field above."

"The devil mend you," said Meleanthus.

"Do you mind the time," said the white pony, "we ate the coloured straw your master had making baskets?"

"That was a nice man," said Meleanthus. "If he'd a crust of bread, he'd give it you. And if he hadn't, he'd give you a kick, for that was all he had itself. Do you mind his wife?"

"I do then. A harmless poor lump of a

girl could steal a hen without it would cluck
once.   She left him since for a sailing man,
said he was after losing his best finger 'twixt
two ships collided in a battle."

"Do you say so!   And was he a nice
man?"

"He was not then.   But he had the finger
he lost put up in a bottle of spirits.   And
there were gold rings on it.   And she liked
that."

Outside in the rain, the master of the white
pony sat with his family about a brazier.
Round the shoulders of each a sack was
drawn; but because there were a great many,
the two smallest had but one sack between
them.   He took a turnip from the fire and,
when he had cut each a slice, threw the top to
his pony in the dyke.   Meleanthus extended
his lip—and swallowed it.

"It's a queer thing," said the white pony.
"I have a hunger on me would eat the spout
from a brass kettle.   I suppose you'd get
all you're wanting from the man below."

"I would then," said Meleanthus.   "But
a snack here and there's no harm to me."
From the corner of his eye, he watched with
unconcern the red flash of the tinker's knife.

"And what happened her since?" said he.

"They're saying the rings went green as brass. And it's how they told her, he lost his finger snaring rabbits in the glens of Kill. So she went from him then."

In quiet haste, Meleanthus' neck shot out into the briars. "You rascal, you!" cried the white pony. "You took another top on me! Indeed, you're as bad a rogue ever you were."

"Why now!" said Meleanthus in surprise. "Were you wanting it yourself?"

"It's better," he mused, "a man not to have a wife. For if he likes her—tormenting her as it were with praise—she'll sicken of him in a week. And if he doesn't like her, it might be he'll not be quit of her till he has her dead."

Towards the brazier, the laden briars dripped flame.

Many fires were lit upon the Green, revealing, each in its own glow, the heart of some gathered life, where was collected some family or troupe. It was raining faster now, so that about each was a halo of swift-falling raindrops. But in the spaces between was nothing but a soft dusk drifting up the field.

Nearby, the tinker addressed his son.

"Will you go mind the shop for your Ma the way she'll get her supper? You can take a green sweetie from the shelf."

"No-o," said his son.

"Would you go for two sweeties?"

"I would not."

"Or for three sweeties?"

"Then I will," answered his son. And pulling the sack over his head, he ran down the hill; till nothing was seen but that moving pile, and beneath it the twinkle of two feet.

Presently the sack returned. But now there emerged from beneath a pair of boots with big toes and a rent seam. It dropped among the little sacks.

"How many have you there?" asked Meleanthus.

"Last time I counted," said the white pony, "there were seven was in it."

"Now do you like," said he, "travelling the world with that rattery?"

"I like it well," said the white pony. "For they are lively upon the roads. And besides," he said, "when they will go sleep about the fire, they are continually rolling and squeaking and wriggling, and that is company for me in the hush of night."

"I'd not like that," said Meleanthus. "For the world's a troublesome place, and you'd need to think on it a great deal. But with that—chicken-run fastened to your tail, you'd have no leisure but to be knocking them off by day and night."

Above the merry-go-round, the voice of the gaming woman tore at the dark.

"May you choke!" cried the white pony. "You took the last top is in it!"

"Now did I?" said Meleanthus. "I wasn't thinking." And with a pleasant sound, he crunched that juicy flesh.

Footsteps stirred in the grass. Cleran and Keth were returning up the hill. The Saint's horse poked up his head and neighed gently to attract his master; but on being approached, he bit at the night with backward ears to prove he hadn't meant it.

"The devil mend you," he said in farewell to the white pony.

"May he nourish you well," replied his friend.

And so they parted.

As he set out Meleanthus drooped his

ears, as one grown callous with accustomed splendour; for without doubt the eyes of all the horses, of the little ass and the flaming jennet, were upon him. But the black horse did not curvet or rear. For Keth sat limp upon his back and let him be, as if some thought other than he possessed her mind.

"Do you remember," she said, "how we left the circus at Dungarvan, and in the dark your arms were about me suddenly?"

"I do indeed," he said. And he stroked her hand.

She laughed.

"Tell me," she said, "how can it be that in a kiss lightly given there are messages of doom?"

The rain fell softly. The merry-go-round still played its three tunes: merry galloping rhythm, "the Rakes of Mallow," "the Wild Hills of Clare," and again, merry galloping rhythm. It grew faint and vanished down the glen. But still the cry of the gaming woman was a lost wail wandering in the dark.

XIV

AUTUMN

Since Cleran and Keth had left the sea she
had wanted no other company, but guarded
him jealously.

For from that day, there was none so gentle
as he. His eyes, that had stared helplessly
upon her, considered her with a grave concern. He would for ever have been asking
whether she grew tired, whether she were
touched of the cold wind, whether aught
troubled her mind. There were days when
he mused for a long while, then related to her
some tale he had told to his people among the
hills, as if it seemed to him this must bring
her cheer. But, "What is the use?" she
said, "for I cannot understand them. And
as he speaks he does not look at me, so that
his far sad tales lie heavy on my heart."

Did she grow angry, he calmed her as one

might a little child; would she have mocked him, he was only glad because she laughed. And for this, her heart was full of fear. "For what man," she said, "will pity his beloved, till he has forgotten how to pity himself?"

So she kept him jealously. At dusk, when they passed the little houses that invited them with a quiet glow, she would hurry on into the night. While did there creep from a ditch the taint of smoke, and drawing near, they heard the drone of tinkers over a red fire where the little ones huddled half asleep; she would pluck his sleeve, with news of some forgotten hill, and whisper that there alone might they rest undisturbed save by the wandering gentle wind.

For did they but pass a beggar at the roadside, she watched him, how his eyes grew still with the patience that is without hope. And she thought: "Whoever speaks to him by the way, he remembers his people that he left for me among the hills."

They had turned again towards the South when Autumn fell across their path. The leaves of the chestnut grew yellow on the branches and bronze upon the ground;

rain soaked the coloured fern. From each heap of stalks where there were gardens, the blue smoke of Autumn rose into the air.

Yet still she scorned to shelter; for it seemed to her, that only in the small cares and perils of the road might she come close to where he was. He pulled bracken for her bed where the blushing speckled oak-apples peeped from among the leaves. Through the dark leaves fluttered on her white arms, and on the lashes of her eyes.

As they came to the forests of the West and South, the nights grew wild, and rain drove aslant among the turbulent oaks. At this she laughed for joy. He contrived a shelter of wind-fallen boughs; while with the rain brightening her soft cheek, she wove a spray here and there, whispering that now indeed they were proud lovers who cared for one another only. But it was Cleran who dragged up the great boughs.

As for the horses, all night they must stand with hunched backs beneath the sting-ing rain. Because of this the black horse was filled with anger. His rage lasted through the night. It was no less in the morning than it had been at dusk. He would lay flat his ears and shake from his coat the teasing rain; then in a fury he would shift his feet, and stamping, snatch at the drops which so outraged him. All day he'd brood on his grievance of the night, while through the night-time it glowed within him like a fire. For by this means did he contrive to fill his drab life with warmth and splendour.

As for Meleanthus, with head drooped and tail turned to the rain, he pondered deeply:

Whether a person liked to be uncomfortable, or if he was aware of no alternative, but to be bored—

Whether rain were good for the soul or merely made it damp—

And what crabbed genius it was invented women, or whether they had invented themselves—

Till, lulled by these nice speculations, he fell into a dreamless sleep.

It happened one night when they were come to the hills about Caragh and Dunloe, that the black horse broke its tether, and snorting, went where it would among the forests. They sought it the next day in vain. The sound of many waters filled the valleys. In their despair the trees rocked to and fro.

Then the Saint left his beast at the house of some poor woodland folk and set out on foot for the far glens; but when he bade Keth wait for him there, she would not stay. "Let me come with you," she said, "for in your company, I do not feel the rain upon my cheek."

So at his side she set out through the heather, and the frechauns [1] heavy with rain-drops, while overhead the brushing trees swung wearily.

At dusk they thought to distinguish a horse that moved on the far hill-side. But when they would have crossed to where he was, the dark swirl of a stream flowed in their path, on whose flood the last light of day was caught and flickered by.

Then the Saint lifted Keth and carried her through the stream, and in his arms she crouched, well satisfied. "When I am with you," she said, "I am content, though the wind blow. Yet it may be you are not glad I came. Sometimes, I have thought you are

[1] Frechauns : bilberries.

no longer glad to have me at your side."
Below them the flood grew smooth and
narrowing, fled towards a fall. He could
scarcely stand.

Cleran listened to the waters.

The strands of the fall were made of crystal. They rang together in frail chimes,
and their voice was too beautiful for the ears
of men. Beneath them the flood roared—
an unchained terrible music, troubling the
heart. Listening to that song, his spirit
wearied for its own country, where long since
it had heard that which was hidden from
men.

The stream tugged at his knees. And it
seemed to him it had been most sweet to
yield his grip of the sleek rocks, and to lose
in that untravelled beauty the thin ache of
day by day.

"Sometimes," said Keth's vain voice above
the waters, "I think your face is sad. I do
not know why, but I am troubled, looking at
your face."

The Saint plunged to the looming bank
and, laying her among the fern, dragged
himself ashore. Then because it was dark
he built a fire, while flitting here and there

she brought him little twigs such as a mouse might carry, and smiled shyly up into his face, to see if he were glad.

The clouds had parted, and amid the small shock of branches they seemed to hear the horse crash now and then. He bade her shield the fire that he might go and seek it; and for a while she knelt proudly in the fitful moonlight, and fostered the little blaze against his coming. But soon she began peering among the branches to see where he had gone; so that when he returned defeated, there was nothing left but three charred sticks and a blackened circle in the grass.

That night he dreamed. He saw seven horsemen ride across the sky. While he lay sad on the dark earth, it seemed to him that his spirit rode singing with the horsemen. Where they were the sun had risen already. In the manes of the horses there glistened furtive threads of gold; dust of clouds flew from their feet, and drifted down the edge of day.

Far below, he heard a little sound of weeping. It was himself who wept.

He saw three Seraphim flying up the dawn. They did not move their wings.

As with a swallow in its dive, their tapering slender wings were closed. No power bore them upwards but the power of the ecstasy of song.

The Seraphim faded into light. They were the rose of morning beyond the unawakened hills. And looking back to the dim earth, he saw that there were two who wept.

They wept because but one had wings.

Next day he discovered the black horse with his rein caught in a bush. And returning by some other path, they continued their journeyings, by Mallow, by the Knockmildowns and the long Comeraghs, and eastward to the hills of Leinster.

So Autumn passed.

XV

SNOWSTORM AND DAFFODILS

One night when they walked at dusk among the lonely hills, a snowstorm took them unawares, so that the path faded from before them, and through the night they wandered without mark.

Presently he took off his coat, and held it about her shoulders. And travelling thus, she walked beside him in a deep content.

The flakes fell without stir.

"It may be," she thought, "that to-night he thinks tenderly of me. Or is he hating me, so that he says nothing? Perhaps he is wondering why I do not speak."

And Cleran thought: "A year since on Garryknock there was a great fall of snow. The sheep had strayed from a little field, and perished, it might be, in some deep place. The men stumbled through the wind and shouted to one another, but they found no sign. So they came back out of the buffeting night. And in the yard beside the house there was a stir and a trouble of voices, and men's shadows that passed across the door.

" Then I came, and they were glad: and together we went into the storm" . . .

"The flakes are settling on your coat," she said. "I can feel them with my hand."

There was no answer.

"They alight like shy birds on your rough coat. Then their wings droop. And where they were, your coat is wet."

"Dear, you are cold!" cried Cleran. He drew the coat more closely about her. "Your arms are chiller than the night," he said.

And he thought: "We searched by Shrahagaragh and Lugmore, till Tom Reilly shouted at my ear, how he had seemed to hear a little cry from the Hollow of the Green Moss. So we went down. The wind blew upon the hill, but in the Hollow of the Green Moss there was no wind. When we lit a torch we could see the gentle flakes. And there, in a drift beneath us, the sheep huddled —their fleeces were dark on the pure snow. So we plunged in, and held to our bodies the spent sheep with their panting sides. . . .

"The old men were glad when we brought them to the fold."

They walked in silence through the thickening night.

"In the little houses," he thought, "when there was snow, the windows were muffled before the hour of dark. From the yard the restless cattle would be lowing, till the man of the house went out to quiet them, and to bring them a handful of dry hay from beside the turf-stack in the shed of stones: you would not hear him come back across the yard. When he lifted the latch he stamped his boots. Then the woman brought in the lamp, and before her the shadows of the men stretched out and climbed upon the wall."

"It grows colder," she said. "It may be we are alone upon the hill. It may be, for three miles or four, there is none other only you and I."

"If I did but know of some house or shepherd's hut," he said, "I could find you warm lodging for the night."

"It does not matter," said Keth. "For the wind is gentle. And there is no sound, only our steps."

But he put no meaning to her words.

"You must be near spent," he said. And they trudged onwards.

Suddenly they began to stumble among loose stones, while about them the wind dropped. Close against her face, dim faces stared. "It is a wall of stones," said Cleran. They felt their way beside the wall: the earth grew rough beneath their feet, as if many cattle had passed that way. Then the night became darker where they were. And putting out their hands, they found in their path a greater wall; but in its side there was the gap of a window, and the sounding, hollow space of a door of wood.

When they knocked at the door there came no answer but a low rythmic sound. They raised the latch, and suddenly there smote on their faces the warm smell of cattle, that within were munching quietly.

"It is the cowshed," said Cleran. "The farm-house cannot be far off."

"Do not let us travel further," she said. " For it might be we should be lost again in the black night. And here is shelter for you and me."

So they went in and closed the door. As they passed behind them, the cows stirred and ran their ponderous chains against the racks. The wind, which had seemed so quiet upon the hill, whistled among the boards. Cleran turned back with hand outstretched. "Dear, are you behind me?" he said. In his strong palm he enclosed the small chill of her hand.

It was quiet in the last stall. Knowing it empty, they went in and sank down in the crisp straw. He covered her with his coat ; while gathering the sweet straw in his arms, he made a pillow for her head. "I would," he said, "you had some better lodging this cold night." For his thoughts were full of anxieties and little schemes for her content. But of herself, that was near him in the night, he did not think.

Then wearily she laid down her head, till with an ache at her heart she fell asleep.

The first time she awoke, she lay shuddering for a long hour, for she thought that she had heard a cry.

"Some creature perishes of cold," she said. And she fell to thinking how she alone, being of the proud Immortals, need not fear the chill of night; since, having served none, she must not die.

"And yet," she said, "it were a lonely thing, one to go proudly to the end of time."

In the next stall, a cow was coughing now and then. The packed snow was slipping on the roof, until it seemed to her that many presences moved about that place.

"Strange it were," she said, "to serve the man that was your own, scheming for his joy only; and it may be, death to come gently in your way, the time you might grow a little tired with the length of the long years."

Then the cry came again. And trembling, she turned her face into the wall.

The next time she awoke the cow still coughed; but through the cracks in the boards there glimmered the faint light of dawn. Then out of the distance a cock crowed. And she was comforted.

When she awoke for the last time, it was broad day. From the stalls there came the ring of pails, the expectant lowing and the stamp of cows.

She raised the coat and crept out from beside him. Yet she did not wake him. For she had come to fear his eyes when first, from the edge of sleep, they looked at her unmasked.

She heard a stool grate upon the floor.
And from where she was, she perceived two
men who moved among the curled silken
backs of cows that were caked with mud.
The snow was thick upon their boots.   From
their mouths, and from the froth-white milk
in its pail beside the door, steam rose on the
chill air.

They spoke to one another.

"Hurry now, for the gate is blocked
above."

"It's by that way you would bring in the
ewes?"

"Isn't it as well," said a third voice, of
whom no more was apparent than two hands,
which drew from under a cow's flanks the
sweet keen arrows of the milk, "to bring
them soon into the yard?   For the roof is
fell in from the haggard was beneath the
wall."

"I suppose she'll never mend."

"That is a thing you couldn't say.   But
it is a pity, the first lamb to have perished on
us.   Only the like of two tremors did he give,
and there was he hanging from my hand like
a rag on the briar of a bush."

"If it happened some cow-doctor would go

by, or a holy man with his charms and with his prayers, he might recover her so."

"There are no holy men," said the voice. "For what is in this land, only flighty ignorant young people, and girls do go coaxing and whispering at the fall of night?"

"They are saying, a man to have gone by in Kiltealy a while since was a great Saint out of Wicklow and the East."

From beneath the belly of the cow there rose a mocking bitter laugh.

"Is it a Saint?" said the voice. "Sure if that one's only a man yet, he should thank God for it. Ranging through the land he is at the heels of one you'd turn from in the night, knocking your shins among the bushes, and putting crosses in the air before you."

"And he a terrible man, so they say, for cures and for wonders in the days gone by!"

"Yet a person to be a Saint itself, wouldn't he have reason to take his share of pleasure now and then?"

"Pleasure is it!" cried the voice. "Isn't he only fretting day and night after what he left? Killed dead he is, going this way and that by the knocks, and by the hidden roads, the way he'll flee the scorn of men. But there's no doubt that with her spells she'll keep him sick or sane till the day he'll be stretched before her in his grave."

Then Keth shrank back. And in a little while she heard the men go from the shed.

Cleran came out from the stall behind her. She glanced at him, but he did not look her way. "Let us go," he said. And he brushed past her.

They came into the blinding day.

And stumbling as they went, they passed the gate, and set out in haste through the white fields. They staggered through drifts. The staring snow clung to their heels. And it might be for an hour or more they did not speak to one another.

Winter passed by, and still they travelled on.

On the hill-sides, the woods of Shillelagh stirred with Spring. The tree-tops were purpled of new buds. They were a rolling plain where sunshine and cloud chased one another. They lived at the sun's touch— were darkened of mock frowns, and flushed of virginal slow smiles. Streams flashed.

From the dead leaves one primrose poked its head, and waited, shining without fear.

They had touched the fringe of Wicklow: he did not know for what whim she led him by that way. "We will go by the coast to Dublin," she said. And all the while she whispered in her heart: "He will look at his sad hills, and will pass by. It is not true, what they say. We will leave them in our path, and go laughing to Northward at the heels of Spring. And I will know then that it is not true."

One evening as they rode among the meadows, they came to a hollow where Lent lilies flowered. Their pale petals were grown limp with dew; in each yellow throat a dew-drop rested. They did not grow in scattered tribes, but as it were in towns and gay communities. Their little faces crowded in the grass. Some were modest, some innocent and enquiring. Some twinkled in merry groups; some, with drooped heads, mused singly and apart.

So these two loosed their packs. And spreading their rugs in the deep grass, they made their camp where they might look on that new loveliness.

"Are they not beautiful?" said Cleran. "To-morrow," he said, "we will be sad to leave them here. I would their bright faces might come with us to cheer us through the winter days."

She watched him with her anxious eyes.

"It would make you glad?" she said.

Then Cleran reproached himself. For he thought: "I am no more to her than a morose and hollow-eyed companion."

"Dear," he said, "I have you. What more do I need to make me glad?"

"What more?" said Keth. And her voice was without joy. "Yet sometimes," she said, "your eyes will look on a far place. And to-day, when I spoke to you, you answered softly, yet your answer had nothing to do with the thing of which I spoke."

At that he laughed. And tenderly, he told her all she most would hear, so that she was a little comforted.

But next morning when day crept among the trees, she rose from the crushed warm grass where they had lain. With a little laugh, she looked upon his sleeping face; then stole among the daffodils.

They were a faint gleam in the grass. She

stooped down and, holding out her dress, began to pluck them hastily. She pinched them off close beneath the head—for she was unversed in the gathering of flowers—and dropped them into her skirt. Beginning at the edge, she picked her way through each dim company till it was blotted out. Then she began upon another.

The dew-drops grew chill about her ankles. Before long her back started to ache, but she did not care. She panted as she worked, the limp heads were bruised in her hot palms.

Over the drenched tangled grasses the trees were waiting for the dawn. In a tree-top some brave bird put out three notes, and was answered from far distances. Light warmed the flowers in her dress. And seeing that crush of gold, Keth laughed for joy.

When she had finished, the hollow of the field was dark. At its far end one flower, that in her haste she had forgotten, twinkled in the dawn.

She turned. And coming timidly to Cleran, she touched him on the shoulder.

Cleran awoke, and saw the battered flowers. In their misfortune they had assumed a rakish appearance, their petals cocked this way and that. "What have you done?" he said.

"Look," said Keth. And she held out her dress.

"Oh," he said, "it is too much! Have you no thought in all the world but to destroy, and to destroy again?"

"They are for you," she whispered. And her mouth drooped.

He turned from her. "Had I asked you to kill beasts or men, you would have done that also, were it your whim to make me smile. Ah, why," he said, "were you made thus without a heart?"

She stood shivering in the stark light.

Then she ran from him. And when presently he went to seek her, he found her weeping among the grass. While about her the scattered flowers regarded the sky with patient eyes.

XVI

HE LIGHTS A FIRE

IT was cold. The naked boughs of Avoca did not stir. The sky was the colour of steel.

They came as the day waned to a place where the roads parted; for one ran down into the valley, where here and there a light already shivered, the other onward into solitude.

When they reached the cross, Cleran hung back. "It is Patrick's night," he said. "Let us go to the village: for there will be firelight upon the panes, and men will be gathering from the townlands and talking of old times."

She did not move, but stood where he might not see her, looking at his face.

"Let us go to the village," he said. "For it is silent here."

She answered bitterly: "The trees are
157

listening for our words, and yet we do not speak, but shiver as we go."

"It is as you will," he said gently. And they turned toward the night.

In a little while the trees grew thin, and between them could be seen the dim extent of moorland.

"Let us make our camp here, where there is still shelter," he said. And when he had unsaddled the horses, they stooped among the frozen beech-leaves and gathered brittle twigs for a fire.

The trees were silent. Upon the tips of the branches, tender shoots of green looked strangely on the world.

Cleran put a match beneath the twigs. The little flame sprang up bravely; but perceiving the desolate night, it shuddered, and went out. He struck again. The flame lurked, gathering out of sight. Frail pioneer, a thread of smoke set out for the chill sky.

At this signal there was a tiny scuffle of bare feet, and two children peeped from behind a tree with their big eyes. They peeped again: then hopped nearer across the leaves like little birds.

"But who are these?" cried Cleran.   And Keth watched how his eyes had lit.

"I am Eugène," whispered the first.

"And I am Me-ary," said the other. Her whisper made so slight a stir that she must needs put her mouth close to his ear.

"And what can it be that brought you to so great a wood?"

"We're looking could we see a rabbut," whispered they. And at this they were filled with so great confusion that each buried its face in the shoulder of the other.

"Listen," said Cleran.   "A rabbit is for every day.   But to-night it is Patrick's night, and we are about to make a feast." He laid his hands on their spare shoulders. "Will you be my messengers?" said he.

"We will," they whispered.

"Then Eugène, you must go to the next farm—or it may be you have a farm your-selves—and find me the biggest goose that ever walked across the world, and bring him to me here.   And Mary, you shall bring me a cake of wheaten bread, and from the dairy a lump of butter that is as big as my two hands."   And taking from his pocket four silver coins, he put two into the palm of each.

The little ones arose and, squeezing the coins in their hot hands, they scuttled out of sight. For a while, a leaf stirred where their feet had rested. Then nothing was heard but the fire cracking.

Presently Keth was aware of two forms which moved among the trees. A man and his wife were gathering sticks. Their footfalls made no sound: and though they would sometimes meet together and lay down their sticks on a little pile, they did not speak to one another.

Keth saw that Cleran was watching them. She perceived too that he felt relief, because there were others in the wood besides themselves. In a moment, as had seemed to her inevitable, he left her side that he might speak with them.

"It is a cold night to be abroad," he said.

"Isn't it only the best thing," said the man, in a voice of gentle melancholy, "a person to be cold to-day; and death that is before him the one day, or the other day, and it may be a fire will roast him to the end of time?"

He came into the firelight, so that the glint of copper, of gold and of a sanguine flame, leaped in his red hair. From the corners of his mouth there dropped two sorrowful moustaches; while without reverence, at the tip of each, an icicle winked.

The fire was now a grateful sight. Along the frailer sticks little tongues ran, and nodded in a row. At its heart the great boughs had caught, so that a curtain of flame hung high above the earth.

"It may be," said Cleran, "that in Heaven, too, there are fires, and the Lord of Heaven bidding them pile high the sticks to cheer our hearts."

He turned, and perceived the eyes of Keth fixed mournfully upon him.

"Beloved," he cried, "come quickly! Is it not good to light a fire!"

And, as she ran to him eagerly: "Come, you too," he cried to the others. And at that the light left her face.

The woman drew near out of the trees, and, crouching, shivered before the fire. With a creaking of many joints, the man sat down. "In heaven there is nothing," said he, "and in hell there is nothing, but a great torment, or it may be a grandeur would kill you altogether." And with a sigh, he clasped his hands about his knees.

The icicles began to melt.

Out of the dusk, the little ones returned. Mary held in her arms a cake of bread which was almost as big as she. Eugène dragged the limp body of a goose across the leaves. Its beak was open, so that its tongue stuck out foolishly.

When he reached the fire he let it fall, and brought from his coat a packet of butter that had been squeezed to a strange shape.

"Indeed," said Cleran, "you have killed me a fine bird."

" 'Twasn't I," whispered Eugène. " 'Twas Micky cot her."

And since Cleran did not ask: "And who is Micky?" he must continue at his ear. "He is a wonderful man," said Eugène. "He has killed a madman with a skivver. And he has drunk two barrels of porter in the one night."

"A man had two heads killed his daddā," whispered Mary, "and he ran after him three nights and three days."

"He was serving with the King of Asia," said Eugène. "But now he'll stop wid us digging spuds, the way he'll put the strength into his arrum will stretch the man killed his dadda.''

Cleran took the goose, and showed them how it might be wrapped in clay and put to bake beneath the fire. And as he did this, he smiled with shy pride at his accomplishment. ''If you look in the saddle-bags,'' he said to the children, ''you will find what is needed for our meal.''

At this there were footsteps on the road, and two stone-breakers drew near, returning from their work. One was rugged as the stones he quarried. But the other was young and gentle in his speech.

They drew near to see what might be afoot.

''Have you a pot to bile the tea?'' said the younger. ''For we have a nice pleasant little can.''

Cleran had a pot. But he borrowed the can: for he knew how a person will delight to lend his peculiar possessions. ''Though now we have your can,'' he said, ''you also must stay and share our meal.''

There was a stir beyond the fire, and Keth rose to her feet. ''I am weary,'' she said. ''I would rest awhile.''

He scanned her face. "Dear," he said, "I'll miss you at my side. Stay but to help me. . . ."

"I am weary," answered Keth. And—as he would have risen—"You need not come with me," she said. And she went apart among the trees.

The young man stared after her, seeing none else. "Glory of Heaven!" said he.

"Now," said the old stone-breaker, "if this isn't the best night iver we struck!" The children were busy about the fire, bringing out plates and pewter mugs that rang together. The boughs fell in with joyous cracks. Two paces distant, the night crouched, sullen and impotent.

The goose was cooked. There came from it a smell that was like the smell of gardens in July; it was like the sound of bees droning in the sunlight; it was like the colour of the sun upon dead leaves. Cleran lifted it from the fire and the clay came neatly away with the feathers, disclosing its succulent dark flesh. And when he had cut bread from the loaf, he began to carve it skilfully and, laying a portion upon each slice, to deal it out among the company.

"That's a fine bird he killed," said the young stone-breaker of Eugène.

"It wasn't I," whispered Eugène. " 'Twas Micky cot her."

"I knew a goose," said the other, "and she was no bigger than the goose was killed by Eugène there, and she give a puck to a man knocked the eye out of his head the way he didn't get it again till the next day."

"I know a grand song," said the woman suddenly, "of two geese did fly across the world, and they were a prince and a princess."

"Woman," said her husband, "what do you know of songs and singers?"

His wife glanced at him guiltily and relapsed into a modest silence. The talk dropped dead as at a blow.

Then a voice rose out of the night.

"She had a stiff neck," said the voice, "and a contrary mind, but I'll take my oath there is flesh of silk upon her bones."

They looked up and saw a man of rugged appearance, in whose eyes the fire leaped roguishly. It was Micky.

"Well, now," said the stone-breaker, "if this isn't the man did break that haughty neck!"

At this the woman laughed delightedly. But remembering her husband, she threw him a glance and became silent.

The children looked at Cleran. "That's Micky," they said. But their words implied: "A hero has come. Yet you sit still and make no sign!"

Cleran cut the last wing from the goose and, laying it on bread, bade him be seated. Micky took the wing. Yet he did not begin at once to eat it. But taking his seat among the leaves, he gazed thoughtfully upon it.

"I knew a fattened goose in Tobin-Toller," he said slowly. "And I took her neck in my two hands, and knotted it in three knots, and there was she still pleasant and lively and looking at me there wid her face."

The company looked ruefully at each other, as if they would say: "Now why could we not have thought of such a tale?" The children, too, exchanged glances. And their glance said: "Now we shall hear some talk worth listening to"

"And what is it did she do then?" whispered Eugène.

"She unknotted her neck then.   One knot first, and then another.   And when she had the t'ird knot out-ravelled, she went from me there upon the hill-side with the walk of a young queen."

He stared down at the wing of the goose and began to bite it thoughtfully at one end. "They are a strange bird and full of peril," said he.

The red man had paid no heed to this narration.   In fact he seemed unaware of all that passed around him.

"Woman," he said suddenly to his wife, "where have you your knowledge of songs and singers?"

The woman looked to Cleran in a small flutter.   "That is a great man for the fiddle," she said.   "For he has a melodious nature, and a violinsome nature; and it's maybe he'd not like it, I to meddle with his tunes and with his songs."

"She have no taste," said the man, "and no liking for that sort of thing."

"Did you ever ask her?" said Cleran.

"'Deed," said the man, "and I hardly spoke to her, since the day they brought her to the church and married her to me there."

"'Two people,'" said the woman, "to be living together in a lonely place, what way is it they would be talking, but one to say, 'Will you go fetch me a drop of spring water for the tea?' and another to ask, 'Did you bring in the red cow from the hill?'"

"I knew a couple," said Micky, "and they were married ten years, and hardly a word that passed between them. And the man was as bald as a brass nail. But one night the woman give him a sort of close look, and she said to him: 'Isn't it a pity now, your beard not to be growing, the place you should be keeping the hair of your scalp!' And at that he up and kilt her with a hatchet."

"Speech," said the red man, "is sometimes a good thing, and it is sometimes a bad thing, and it is sometimes only a frisking of the tongue is neither good nor bad."

"But if, the time he was abroad," she said to Cleran, "I took down the fiddle and played a jig upon it, or 'The Wild Geese,' or 'Jerry, hold your Talking,' it is no harm that I did itself."

The man looked dolefully at the fire. "She couldn't play 'Jerry, hold your Talking,'" said he, "for there are none could play that tune, only them that have drink-taken."

He stopped. For it seemed a great company drew near among the trees.

"Bestir yourselves, all of you," rang a proud female voice. "You are grown too slow altogether. Bring on the food and the drinks! Will you not stir up the horses and the little asses and the mules! What's this? Is it through the night that I will wait? Faith, and you'd say I was no-thing itself, but a woman came begging from the hills!"

The din drew nearer.

"Is it for this I put you in speckled livery, to ride upon cloths of gold? Look now to the nine white horses! I do hear them astray among the glens, and the jewels of Shiks and of Shauhs that are jostling there upon their sides. Faith, I'll have you disintegrāted, the whole crowd of you. Isn't it plates of gold you are bringing, and flagons, and mugs are alive with little jewels, and will you scatter yourselves across the world?"

The listeners strained forward. So edged were their imaginations, that they thought to hear the beat of many hoofs, and to catch a glint of gold here and there among the trees. Then into the firelight came one small figure that dipped and peered this way and that. It was the Countess Corrigan.

She stopped, dazed by the fire's light.

"The feast is ready," said Cleran. "There is no need to wait."

Still she looked at the ground, fiddling with her skirt.

"It were an honour," he said, "to entertain such company."

She drew herself up with a gesture. "Ah, not at all," said she. "Don't be talking now, for I'll not heed you."

At that they arose as one man and made room for her at the fire. They laid what was left of the goose before her, and put tea at her elbow in a shining mug. She sat down, bowing to left and right.

"Good company I am in," said she. "For isn't it quality that I see about me, and no common people, did rise like nettles from a load o' muck?"

They lifted the shining mugs and drank. In the side of each mug a miniature fire leaped and curled.

"Indeed," said Micky, "that's the right company for yourself."

"Arrah!" said she, "for the rest, I wouldn't notice them. Tradesmen that do strut the town, without ease, without cursen' or squanderen'. Low common little men knocken' around, couldn't tell the poll of a horse from the tail be-hind it." She raised the mug high. "I that came from the hills to sup with lords, and with Holy Men did walk the world!"

"Are you come by Contha and Knockalt?" said Cleran. And his face clouded.

She leaned close to him.

"The very same," whispered she. "And not a man that's in it but is killed dead, crying for yourself."

"That's it," said Micky. "Aren't they laid out like wasps with the harsh winter that went over them, hadn't its like since Noah made matches in the Ark of God?"

Cleran grew troubled. "Tell me," he said. . . .

"Well, you remember Tom Quin of Lug-golash. Didn't a wakeness come on him in the night, and he ups and takes a draught of porter from the shelf, and not a stir out of him after, but his spirit going from him and you couldn't say where that went itself."

"What was Mag doing?" cried Cleran. "Didn't she remember what I said . . ."

"And then Nannie Quailey, isn't she very bad?   Faith, it's the world has her destroyed. Too great a hacking she got altogether, with her man had the use went from his limbs, and not one she'd cry crack to, only herself.   It's how they're saying, she'll not be better till she's dead."

While the talk went thus, the red man sat with his eyes turned in upon themselves; and it did not seem that he heard a great deal of the conversation.

"Now isn't it a queer thing," he said: "two people to be rising together, and digging spuds together, and supping together off inions, and off cabbages, and off the bit of pig they hung itself, and they to be no more acquainted than two bloody turnips did rise up in the one furrow of a field?"

"You are silent," said Cleran, "because you have never spoken.   There is only one silence without remedy, and that is the silence when one has spoken too much."

"Now, do you say that?" mused the red

man. And as he considered his wife, it happened that she raised her head, so that they remained for a long time in rapt contemplation of one another.

"Now you remember that fine lump of a gerrl," said Micky, "you cured of the histrionics in Granogue."

"Yes?" said Cleran.

"She took to them again, the time you couldn't see the dykes for snow. Didn't she go roaring through the world, the way they found her stretched dead in Glenamahl, and her eyes that were open to the sky?"

"But they should have talked reasonably with her!" cried Cleran. "To quiet her was no hard thing, though fear should make her mad."

"And who is it that would quiet her?" said the young stone-breaker in his gentle voice. And looking into his eyes, Cleran saw how they too were the eyes of a man out of the hills.

"The old people?" he asked. "What has become of Michael Dolan, and of John Lalor out of Glenmalure?"

"He died too," said Micky. "Didn't the

lungs go perish on him, and not the bray of
an ass of straw 'twixt the clouds of God and
his own bed, only five sticks and a sod of
grass?"

The Countess moved close to him. And
of a sudden she seemed to him horrible.
"Low common people," said she, "dying
in their beds, while great lords are riding
through the land." She began to shout.
"Gold in their pockets, silver in their fists.
. . . What's that?" said she.

A twig had snapped in the dark behind
them. They turned and saw how Keth
stood listening, white in the dim wood.

There was a long silence.

"Well, then," said Micky, "didn't you
give us a grand night of it? And now,
isn't it time we quit itself, for it's how they're
saying: 'One the bats know well, the devil
will know after.' "

The rest rose with him.

"That's it," laughed the old stone-breaker.
"A quiet man, isn't he better in his bed than
out of it?"

"Is it thim little bats?" whispered the
Countess. And swaying to her feet, she
peered into the night.

As they went one by one, the young stone-breaker remained, and gazed at Keth. "Glory of Heaven!" said he, "is it you took him?"

"I take from men all they have," said Keth.

And at that he turned and went after the others.

The fire had sunk to ticking ashes. There was nothing left of the feast but, here and there, a scattered crust, and the head of the goose with its dead eyes.

"If you went back to your own people," said Keth, "you would be welcome."

He faltered. "I do not know. . . ."

"Yet I know," she said, "what is in your mind. Alone, you would be more than welcome. But if I should come with you, they would drive you from the doors with stones."

XVII

THE MOON SAILS BY

Early and late she was silent, watching him.

"When first he came to me on the bridge," she said, "he was proud and full of joy. The light of the sun laughed in his face. Now, in his face there is no joy. There is pain only—and patience. And this is pain to me also, I do not know why."

They had halted for the night by a little wood of oaks and birches. While he made ready their meal she did not help him, but sat with idle hands among the leaves. Her fingers plucked at every leaf. They searched in the rough moss, pulling the ice-smooth acorns from their cups, and crushing the bossed cups to powder.

She saw him unload the packs and take out what was in them, and lay the fire in a sheltered place. And all these things he did with a terrible precision, as if their importance must not be forgotten. "If he went back into the hills," she said, "he would be once more a king and go proudly on his way. The shadow of patience would have left his face."

He looked up and smiled at her, and the kindness of that smile was a prick pointed sharper than ill words. "Come," he said, "and we will eat."

They ate their meal together. But when they had finished, she lay wearily back among the fern and did not look at him.

"My dearest, you are tired," he said. "Your head aches." And putting water upon the fire, he gathered for her such herbs as he knew well how to mingle, and began to bathe her head with his quiet hands.

"You are kind to me," she said bitterly. "I think it is because you pity me."

He ordered his glance and looked into her eyes. "I have told you," he said, "that I am but awkward and ill-versed in the small ways of love. But I will care for you always, and keep you safe from every harm."

"What is love?" she asked him.

"It is to forgive," he answered. And he

continued to bathe her head with his quiet hands.

At length she lay so still that he believed she slept. And when he had put all in order, he too lay down, and dreaming, forgot the monotony of day.

She lay staring up into the night. The moon came up and sailed across the sky, untroubled of men's little cares.

Then rising, she went into the wood, and stood alone. The trees were of an awful whiteness. But one was hidden by another from the moon, and that tree was black as ink.

"If I were not here," she said, "he would go back into the hills. And I would know then that his heart was glad. Were that not enough, to know him glad?" And there rose within her a dull rage. "What woman, being gone," she cried, "desires the joy of her beloved? Rather would she have him broken—pitiful, maimed because of her —lest her fainting heart whisper without warning: 'Does he grow cold?'"

The moon sailed on across the sky. From the roots small animals peeped out, and emerging, played silently in the rapt light. Long after, she remembered how they played. In the shadows they were grey and creeping; in the long beams, sharp mites that darted, or sat up, listening intently. All this was printed on her mind. Though now she did not notice them.

"A hundred years," she thought, "I have served none, lest I should be as men, whom death takes, coming when it will." And at that she shuddered in the night. "Death is cold," she said. "Yet in death there is no grief. The heart is not lonely, resting locked about with the clay of earth."

The shadows had moved from North to East. In the heavens each star changed its post as, at the unhurried motion of one Mind, worlds moved on their appointed way.

"The news would go round," she said, "that he had come back. They would run from the glens and gather at the bridges, and where the roads meet from Glenamahl and from the Gap. He would ride among them with his head high. They'd send up a shout as he drew near." And in the darkness she heard them shout, as you might

see a bright picture framed in the room
beyond the door.

"Yet there would be Togher between us
then, and Curragh plain, and a thousand
fields where men toil, and drive their plough
through the soft earth, and have not heard
of him or me."

The round of the night had run its course.
Constellations sank and waned. Once more
the mind of man was turned back to earth,
till, no longer matched against the heavens,
he thought that he was king.

Presently the trees, that had been of the
pallor of silver, were turned to the pallor
of steel. The shadows too dimmed across
the world, leaving it derelict. Then Keth
looked up, and saw how the moon was a sail
adrift in a wan sky, bereft of its small craft
of stars.

And suddenly she uttered a low cry.

"What can I do?" she said. "For it has
come upon me that I love him better than
myself."

XVIII

THE MOTHER

THEY mounted the long glen.

"Now what is she doing," said the black horse, "bringing him by this way?   To lead him here among his own people!   How does she know she'll draw him from them with her wiles again?"

Meleanthus flicked his ear.

"With a woman," said he, "you couldn't tell what she was at.   The thing she's after, she'll run from it; and the thing she doesn't want, won't she choke you with it day and night till your lip will be curling at the sight of it?"

Spring was come to the dark glens.   Here and there over the hill-sides, and the white cabins stained of dripping thatch, the sunlight drew its healing fingers.   In a larch-wood the trees were tipped with living green.

But some lay stretched one across the other, and on these there was no bud of green.

The valley was still and made no sign, like a woman who has suffered.

"Such a commotion as there was," said the black horse, "the time she put the saddle on me—

" 'We'll go,' she said, 'and look at your sad hills to-day.'

" 'Oh no,' he said, 'I will not do that. Let us make our way to the roads of Dublin, where the chestnuts will be budding already. And there, we'll hear the gay birds and think of Spring.'

"But she answered that they would do no such thing. 'What are you doing,' said she, 'going by without asking for your people? It may be that you are afraid!'

"And she laughed, mocking him."

"A woman to be crying," said Meleanthus, "or to be letting fall six tears or seven, you wouldn't mind her. But a woman to be laughing, she's maybe considering would she split your throat, or it might be knock the world to bits and go scatter it to the stars."

Indeed, it seemed that Keth was in a merry mood.   It was long since her heart had been so light. She teased the black horse, turning him to and fro across the ditches and the perilous shallows of the bogs, and made mock of those whom they passed at their work among the fields—of their hats, of their drooped skirts or the long tails to their coats.

As for Cleran, his mood was ill-attuned with hers. For that day at noon, as he went a little apart to draw water at a green spring, a man and his young wife had come to him by the road. The woman walked with her shawl about her as if she were a queen. And the stillness in her face was terrible. When the man saw him, he came running, and bowed his head to the Saint's hand. "Glory be to God," he said, "you to be here! It is now I am come out to find you, after them saying since last night you were in these parts. For indeed I have my share of trouble."

Cleran remembered him. For in all the glens there was none so gentle as he. Gentleness was in his presence as beauty in a flower. He was but a small man. No assertion of bravery went with him; he held no shining weapons to guard the secrets of his heart. He had this only—that he was gentle.

"Alas Landy," said Cleran, "what can I do for you? For I am not what I was."

The woman stood apart and did not speak.

"It is since she had the little child," said Landy. "Strange she is now and distant in her mind, as if she wouldn't know me. And it's the queer notions she'll have too—she to be some great lady, or one that is higher than the rest." And he looked upon the ground.

"Tell me," said Cleran, "what is on her mind."

"Queer things they are," replied the man. "Indeed, God forgive me if she's not thinking the young child to have been the Lord of Heaven, did come back to take sorrow from the world." He changed his voice to a tender key. "Come here to me now," he said, coaxing, "and speak yourself to the holy man."

The woman drew her shawl about her. And standing where she was, she spoke in a colourless far voice, as one would repeat a lesson learned by heart.

"What did I do," she said, "this great

thing to come upon me? I to bring light into the valley. I to bring him back to the dark valley, that is the Light of Heaven.

"Didn't they tell you that? It's Spring it is from this out. Not to be winter any more. Poor people not to be hungry. A harvest of hay in the bog meadows, and the sun to dry them: fine cocks settled in a row, without you would be looking for the shadow of rain upon the wind.

"Didn't they tell you that? How I brought him back into the valley, that left us this long time in the dark wind?"

"It is the great hardship she had," said the man, "the little one to be dying on her that came to her in the storms of winter. Dazed in her mind she is, the way she'll not hearken how she never seen him; for it's dead he was at the rise of day, and the light of the window that fell on him, coming from the East."

The woman did not hear him. She was smiling quietly by herself. And her smile was colder than the stars of night.

"Little bud," she said. "Little young rose that is come into the world. Soft skies you will bring us; turf coming dry out of the hills, and flour coming plenty from the town. The warmth of the sun upon our faces, and on the wake lambs and the heavy cows. Don't be crying now, my darling that is come to my own house, my little star that is caught in the cradle at my knee."

She turned her eyes to Cleran.

"Only he is so wake and so thin, the little King," she said, and shook her head sadly to and fro. "Poor little scrap," she said, "you to be so thin, that were a king among the shining stars."

"Speaking that way she is by day and night," said he, "since the time the little one is dead."

She stared at him. And her eyes came terrified to Cleran's.

"Do you hear that?" she said. "They are saying he is dead. Then it's a dark world it will be from this out. A dark world and a long rain. Cold ashes on the hearth, white pools upon the road. Trees that are tossed and troubled through the night, and the touch of day too long coming on the window, and on the two posts of the bed."

"What can I do?" said Cleran. "For seeing her so, yet can I bring her mind no ease."

"Couldn't you only say a prayer for her?" begged the man. "For it's how they're saying, that a prayer will lighten the dark mind."

"How shall darkness intercede for light?" he answered, "or the black deep pray for the stars?" And he turned away his head.

"You must go now," he said, "but do not remember ill of me. For to-day I have fathomed the abyss. I can go no deeper."

Then the man took his wife's hand, and these two went upon their way.

"Look!" cried Keth, as they rode through the still evening. "The wind has played with the walls, and tossed the round stones like skittles in the grass. I would I were the wind."

"Yes?" said Cleran.

"It has pulled thatch in tufts from the head of every house. Look! That sallow house where they milk the cows! You would say the rain made sport of them in their beds one night."

"It is a pity," said Cleran, and his voice was low, "such grief to have been while we went our way, forgetting it. Do you not think so?"

Keth laughed. "There is grief enough in every place," said she. "Let us be merry and scorn them that weep."

He turned on her with thin lips.

"Sometimes," he said, "it is hard to be patient with you."

"Those who are sad," said Keth, "should hold their heads high and laugh the more. They are most to be despised who weep."

"You talk wildly," said Cleran. "Your cheeks are flushed."

"Last night," she said, "the moon went to my head like wine."

"It is a pity," he answered quietly, "one to laugh thus, when many are sad."

As they mounted higher the fields ended, and their road set out bravely into the dim bogland; till looking back, they saw how the last farm was lost beyond a shoulder of the hill. But as dusk drew on they came to two fields with broken ditches, and between them the four walls of a deserted house. Twelve beech trees stood in a row beside it.

Because of the west wind they leaned all to the one way; their white trunks were pressed close together, for at one time they had been a beech hedge.

Here the travellers halted for the night. To-day it was Keth who unsaddled the horses. Never till now had she been so deft. She laughed as she worked; her limbs moved with a young pride.

The Saint stood watching her, his dark thoughts far from where she was. Once he stooped to unloose a strap, but his fumbling hands failed at their task. She came near and loosed it for him, then proudly smiled into his face.

When they should have eaten, he still lingered beside the roofless walls, a shadow upon his brow. Then Keth undid the packs and began to arrange them in the house. Here the grass, that outside was cropped of straying sheep, grew long and ragged with weeds. There were two rooms, but the wall between them was fallen nearly to the ground. She spread out the blankets in the inner room. The mugs and plates she ranged upon a ledge of wall, from whose crannies small plants crept and flowered.

In the hollow grate were strewn the rusted tips of many heels, as if a cobbler had once hammered his shoes beside that fire. She gathered a few sticks. And when the fire was lit, she put the kettle on to boil.

There was no more to do. She stood still, and her face was empty of laughter. At length she turned and came to Cleran. "I put the fire in the grate," she said, and glanced at him with her wan smile.

As they went in, the house seemed more desolate, now that from the chimney smoke crept stealthily.

Then while the water boiled, she sat close to him and laid her head upon his shoulder. "Do you love me?" she asked.

He thought still of his people. "I have loved you too well," he answered.

"Yet your love was sweet to me," she said. And for a while she rested where she was, and closed her eyes.

Then she rose and began to move the saddles, that she had thrown down carelessly in the field, and to lay them against the outer wall.

Cleran watched her.

"Dear," he said, "you had best bring them

inside where we are sleeping, lest some tinker come by in the night."

"Must I carry them again?" she said.

Then Cleran went to move them himself.

"Let us leave them there," pleaded Keth. "I have put them thus with the bridles all in a row. I would leave them where they are."

She held his arm. He thought angrily: "Must she cavil thus upon small things, when everywhere there is grief, and we do nothing?"

And he brought in the saddles, laying them close beside his bed, and hung up the bridles in the outer room.

It was so dark now that she could scarcely see him when he moved. Now and then in the field the horses stirred, stamping a hoof. She lingered watching him for a moment. Then turning to her bed, she lay down, and the pity of sleep fell on her tired lids.

XIX

FLIGHT

In the middle of the night she awoke, deliberately, as at a signal. The darkness was thick about her. It lay soft on her eyes and on her hands. She arose and went cautiously into the next room, feeling with the tips of her toes for the stones that might betray her going. She kept her mind carefully upon these—the diminutive contours of the earth, a buried stone where she balanced swaying, the crisp teeth of gravel.

She felt for the bridles and took one down, holding it stiffly by the rings. The snaffle-joints might clink if they hung loose. Then she crept out into the field. She moved still with a scrupulous care, as if this refinement of skill absorbed her mind. Suddenly, she found she had stretched the bit so tightly that the rings cut into her hands.

FLIGHT

The horses were not asleep. She could hear the quiet sound of their teeth tearing at the cropped grass. As she approached they ceased, listening. She touched the shadow of the black horse, and sliding her hand up his mane and down his cheek, attained his pendulous lip. The snaffle grated against his teeth. He drew his head up and back while, glancing at the house, she thought: "He will wake before even I get on the bridle." She was careful to think of him impersonally as an enemy not to be disturbed.

With sly tread she stole back into the house and through the inner door. The saddle lay close above his head. She said carefully to herself: "It is fortunate I can hear him breathing, so that I know where he is lying." His breath must not be warm to her, nor vital. It must be without memories. She slid her hand across the grass and felt for the sharp edge of the leather. Instead, she touched his hand that was flung above his head. She snatched her hand away, and laid hold of the thick, tainted padding of the saddle. The two stirrups might ring against each other or against the buckles of the girths. Struggling back to the horse, she thought without cease of these four entities—the two stirrups, and the two buckles of the girths which must be kept from one another. She did not think of his hand.

As she tightened the girths the horse tossed his head, and the bit rang out like a church bell in a town street. Meleanthus moved uneasily.

She stood, listening. Nothing stirred but a shiver in the trees. Then she slipped the halter from his ears and, placing her foot in the stirrup, swung herself slowly into the saddle. She guided him to the empty road. And moving on to the short grass beside it, she walked him a little way, then gently drove her heels into his sides and urged him to a canter.

She rode for a long while.

By keeping her eyes fixed upon it, she could distinguish the road as a pallor in the grass: but its wraith was continually playing tricks upon her, darting suddenly to one side, or melting into a white mist which rose and lay close against her eyes.

There were gutters cut along the turf at which her horse would prop and lift. She

waited, intent, for this small jar.   She came
to counting his steps between each cut: ten
strides, then a short step, as the next loomed
close beneath his eyes.

Presently she need no longer guess, for
the wan road grew out of the night.   She
looked up and saw two white ghosts, which
were houses, on the hill-side.   Higher than
that she would not look.   The hills lay
infinite and quiet under the dun sky, and to
think of infinity was to think of loneliness.

After another while she dropped her eyes.
The pale grass and the little gutters lay
naked under the dawn's stare.   Then she
drove in her heels.   And urging on the
horse, she began to ride at a great speed—
she knew not whither.

X X

CLERAN

Cleran prepared his solitary meal. The cans rang with a harsh sound between the empty walls

"Strange," he said, " she should ride out so early. For last night it had seemed she was in no wayward mood."

After a while he went into the road, and stooping, traced the prints of the black horse where they turned toward the West. He stood regarding them for a long time. "Yet her moods change," he thought, "as quickly as the sea and sky."

The wind blew softly about his temples. "O mountainy land," said he, "why did I ever leave you?" And with a pensive tread, he walked up the road.

Presently, coming round a bend, he perceived a patchwork of fields on the near hill-side where three white farms were huddled sleepily. Soon he was making his way by a little bohireen that climbed among them.

The mist wandered gently among the fields. It lay thick as yet upon the ditches where, from between the stones, scabious peeped, and reddish frechaun leaves. In the unstirring grass it wove cobwebs and delicate designs.

As he drew near to the first house, an old man came from his door and hobbled to a well of stones in the field below. It was the old man who, last year, had lost the use of his limbs. Now, because his wife was gone, he must creep out and fetch a drop of spring water for his tea. When he had stooped to lower his tin pail, he did not unbend his back, but waited till the clear sweet water should have run in. Then with a little groan he straightened himself out, and rested his pail in the soaked grass.

Cleran went and spoke with him.

"My poor creature," he said, "how is it with you now?"

"Sure, arren't I only shtuck together?" nodded the old man. "And as for my own lovely, beautiful coumerade," said he, "didn't

God Almighty take her from me?" As he turned the door, two great tears ran slowly down his cheeks.

Cleran followed him into the house, and comforted him as best he might. With a kingly gesture, the old man motioned him to the one chair. The pictures which had been tacked so gaily upon the walls, now drooped sagged corners swollen with damp; in far recesses, there was the hunched pile of a bed. A heap of dried boughs lay stranded on the earthen floor. And there was nothing else.

"If I could but come back," thought Cleran. And with a heavy heart he returned again into the morning.

The mist had risen, and lay in a level cloud across the valley where, cut off suddenly by that soft line, there loomed the dark shape of a hill. Across that huge face scarred of little streams, midget sheep grazed on slopes no larger than your finger. One bleated. And in the stillness the sound seemed close to his ear.

Continuing up the bohireen, he reached the gate of a little farm from whose chimney the smoke mounted already. The dogs were not yet awake; but as he placed his hand upon the latch they sprang to life with a furious barking, while their chains ran grating from the shed behind them. "Begone out o' that!" cried a man's voice to the dogs. The door opened, and there came to him the sweet smell of the turf-smoke.

Within, a young woman was baking a cake of bread, while her brother ate his morning meal. Her eyes were grey and half afraid. She had a slow, gentle voice. He was unshaven and threadbare of coat, and smelled of turf and of the hills.

"Oh, you must come in and welcome," said the woman. "For isn't it a wonderful thing, you to be back!"

"I am not come back," he answered. "Alas, I do but pass by upon the road."

The two looked at one another, and they said slowly: "Now isn't that the pity of the world?"

"For all," said Cleran, "I have longed to know how you are faring."

" Sure, haven't the winter us destroyed," said the man, "and the wind that knocked the world to bits?"

"And such a rai-n," said the woman, in her slow voice; "falling day and night, day and night, till it would have you dragged out, it was that slavish.''

"Yesterday,'' said Cleran, "in the lower glens, the sun came out. And they were saying how the wind was changing to the East.''

They considered his words with quiet eyes. "Thanks be to God,'' said they.

Cleran sat at the fire and was content. The woman of the house put her cake of bread into the pan, and hung it among the sods. Covering this with a great slate, she heaped upon it the burning and transparent turf. Then she brought more sods: in the fashion of the mountainy people she built these cold shapes behind the fire, that its red heart should not be chilled.

"It might rain yet,'' said the man. "For yesterday, the time I went after the cows, there was as it were a gloom upon the valley.''

"But isn't it the grand thing himself is telling us, that the wind will change?''

"It is changing already,'' said Cleran. And in that moment his thoughts leaped back to Keth.

The woman stooped and turned her cake of bread. Her brother was looking at the window, upon whose sill there moved a softness that was yet not sunlight. "You said it," he marvelled, "that the day will rise."

Presently she took her cake from off the fire, and laid it upon the table. With a peculiar care she cut a slice, and when she had spread it with saltish butter, brought from the shelf a faded plate.

"Won't you taste it now?" said she. "Sure it would put great heart into you. If you would only use a little slice" . . .

She gazed at Cleran. "You didn't hear me!" said she.

Cleran rose from his chair.

"My own people," he said. "I must be leaving you now. For suddenly many thoughts trouble my mind." And he took their hands.

He went out across the yard—past the pecking hens and the frail, faint flowers—and leaned upon the gate.

"What am I doing?" he thought. "For last night she was in no wayward mood. She was gentle and very quiet. 'Your love,' she said, 'was sweet to me . . .'" He stared at the hard earth. "How should it be," he said, "if she should not come back?"

THE STORY OF KETH

As he descended the bohireen, it seemed that the great ditches hemmed him in, while the unnumbered loose stones delayed his feet. At the first gap he turned into the fields. By now the mist had left the valley, and the dark hill stood unveiled before him. Afterwards, he remembered how its wet rocks were glistening in the morning light. He heard the rattle of a cart as it drew near upon the westward road, and the sound of it maddened his mind. Sometimes it shrieked; sometimes its clamour grew so faint that it seemed to him it would never come. Once it was still for a long while, as if, perhaps, some package had been dropped.

He hurried through the drying grass. As he came into the road, the cart was rattling contentedly towards him.

He saw the untroubled faces of two men, and knew that they were his friends; but in his distress he did not recognize them. They pulled up to bid him welcome.

"Tell me," he said. "Did a young woman—riding a black horse—go by you at dawn of day?"

"We heard tell of that," answered one. "Old John Quin it was, will rise up with his

thoughts and he out upon the hill, the time
the grouse do feed in the young heather.
'Tis he seen her, going to the West. 'Sorrow,
is in that ride,' he said. 'At a great speed
she went by me, and the trouble in her eyes
that was bitterer than the Seas of Moyle.' "

Cleran went slowly back to where his
horse was tethered. He gathered up the
packs and bound them behind the saddle.
Then he leaned his elbows upon its shoulders,
and remained thus for a great while.

"O Keth," he said, "where will I find you
now, whose love I never knew at all? Blind
I was, and your heart crying out to me, the
day you brought me back to my own country. Not a gentle word did I say to you;
you that rode laughing on your way, making
a great mock of grief. Where is it I will
find you now, that I may comfort you?"

He mounted his horse and turned into the
westward road. The cart had halted, and its
drivers talked across the ditch to the young
man from the farm above. "Come back to
us now," they cried as he rode past.

But their voices sank into the morning.

EPILOGUE

In his coloured house beneath the Bridge of Ooler, the old man whom people called the Wise stood in a deep distress. For twenty years he had fished from the Quay before his door. Every evening as the sun sank low, he brought out his single kitchen chair. And as the ripples spread from beneath his cast, delicate as a fish's fin, in his gentle mind were evolved twenty philosophies, by which all life had been turned to charity and, out-witting pain, moved in mild harmonies to its destined goal.

And now, after twenty years, a fish had come to that stream. It had swallowed the bait with a dumb shock, and in a moment, lay quivering on the quay in its last agony. With trembling hands he had extracted the deep-driven hook. For a while he hoped it might survive that wound. But soon it ceased to struggle in his hand; and when he held it in the cool stream, there came from it no sign, but a deep crimson stain that darkened from before its face and was swept away upon the flood.

He entered his house treading softly, because of the stranger who slept within. For if one grown weary with the road should cross that bridge and ask for shelter, he had never yet refused them. Though did they stay a week, he could not afterwards have told you how they looked, his mind being intent upon imaginings more profound.

Within, the house was warm with the shadow of sunlight. He laid the fish on a blue-willow plate and regarded it sadly.

"O bright life," he said. "O jewel that flashed among the eddies, and with a harmless eye pursued your wandering desire. If you snatched a fly, its being was forfeit but to preserve that swift perfection. Alas! to no such end did I——a creature well-fed and indolent——compass your extinction, but for the idle flaunting of my skill. Now the river is dark. And where you were the flood swirls, empty of fire."

From across the bridge his grandchildren

came in, and stood with admiring gaze about the table.

"Isn't he a grand fellah!" said they.

"You must not be rejoiced at that," answered the old man. "For the greater he is, the more years have gone to nourish and evolve that splendour. And thus, the more criminal is this deed."

At that they immediately grew solemn.

"Is he very dead, do you think?" said one.

The next put out his hand, to touch with his finger-tips its protruding eyes and its side speckled of dull red.

"It's terrible dead he is," whispered he.

At that the tiniest peeped above the table, and perceiving that desolate gaping mouth, broke into an impassioned weeping.

"Do not weep," said the old man, "or you will wake her."

The children glanced at the settle, where that warm dusk was quickened of a rarer gold.

"When is it did she come?" said they.

"It may have been yesterday," said the old man. "Or it may have been this morning. I cannot quite remember."

At this they forsook the fish and leaned down, peeping at her heavy lids.

"O-oh, now!" said they. "Isn't she beautiful?"

"I had not noticed," answered he. "But it seemed to me that her spirit was grown weary."

"Did you give her to eat," said the little girl, "the time she came?"

"Indeed," answered the old man, "she would eat nothing at all." And he regarded her helplessly.

"She is panting," said the little girl. "I think that maybe she is very sick."

At that the smallest but one went close and peered into her face.

"Mind yourself now, Timmeen," said the little girl, for being older than the rest she was anxious with authority. "Aren't you too bold, looking so close?

"Let yous come out now," she ordered. "And we'll be gathering flowers for her the time she'll wake. For isn't it best to leave her quiet, and she sleeping?"

They pattered out at her heels. But the smallest but one hung back and whispered at her ear. "I like you better,"

he said, "than anny lady ever I seen."
And like a sly mouse, he darted out into
the sunlight.

The old man stood in the quiet house.
Outside, the sun shone through the creepers,
so that against that enchanted light their
leaves gleamed red. The tendril of one
vine had wandered in through a back window and clung upon the inner wall. It
was forlorn. On the white plaster, by
pictures of holy men and coats or hats
hung upon pegs, it climbed, seeking its lost
sun. But for all its pains it found but the
dim rafters, blackened and sour with smoke.

He went over to where Keth was.

"Indeed," he mused, "they said truly
that she was beautiful. Yet of what more
account her beauty than the fashion of a
leaf or flower? For each gives a like
pleasure to the eye, yet has wrought nothing
of its own loveliness."

At that Keth stretched out her arm and
turned, her eyelids fluttering.

"Oh, I am tired," she said.

"If I remember well," said he, "you have
rested since you came, a night and a day.
Yet still your voice is weary."

"A night and a day!" she said. "And I that a hundred years sought joy, finding no rest. Of what avail one night and one day?"

Outside, the rooks made great clamour across the fields. In busy crowds, they chuckled and shouted to one another. They argued, reproachful or garrulous. Yet the sum of this babel brought to men's minds a sadness as gentle as the long clouds of evening.

"Perhaps," said the old man, "you are one of those from that shadowy place where, through the fingers of the Immortals, joy runs as fine sand. It has been told me that they need but wish and take all things that the heart desires."

"I have all things," she answered, "but the man I love."

"Then you have nothing," he said. "But who is it that would pass by so fair a flower?"

She answered: "I was a torment to him and a despair. I took him from his quiet labour, and from his joy. After that I let him go. And now he is gone back to them again."

"Then," said the old man, "you have all, and more than all. For to take is a little thing. But to give is power, and stillness, and the light of the imperishable ways."

And she answered: "I do not want to be noble and lofty-minded. I do not want the splendour of high thoughts. But I would like to make a fire of sticks with my lover upon a windy hill; he to gather the sticks, and I to cross them upon the flame, and to shield them until he'd come with my two hands. And if he would go a little distance, or it might be beyond a rise of the hill, there would be an empty space in the hour, and a gap in the middle of time. Yet I would say: 'You will look up and see him come again across the ridge of the hill.' "

The old man regarded her helplessly. For his philosophy was so contrived as to prevent all possibility of grief. So that where grief had wrought its way, he was undone.

"I think," he said, "that maybe she is very sick. I will call in the children, for it might happen they could tell what ails her." And he went out.

Keth lay still. The sun had travelled

round the house till its long ray came through the open door. It fell on the motes within the room, making them glimmer and swirl. It fell upon the dresser—on the curve of two plates that did not match, on three egg-cups drawn up proudly, on a row of jugs with their faint flowers and their discreet rims of gold.

She watched these with an idle stare, for to turn her head filled her with a strange weariness. The children's feet padded upon the pathway. She heard their shy whispering at the door; then their shadows crossed the threshold, and the sun shone aslant upon their thin shoulders, and on the tin studs in their little hard shirts.

They flitted to where she was. "Look at now," said they. And into her hand they pressed crushed posies of dandelions, and of crocuses with their blown petals and their sappy stalks.

Keth turned wearily. "Did he tell you to bring me those?" she asked.

"He did not, thin," said they.

"I suppose," said Keth, "he told you you should be kind to me."

"He did not, thin," said they.

"And now," said Keth, "you are afraid of me."

"We are not, thin," said they.

They drew near and fingered her pale hair.

"You don't laugh at all," said they. "Is it because you are that tired?"

"A little since," said Keth, "I was tired. But I think that you have cheered me."

They looked at one another.

"We'll be telling her tales," they said, "for that will make her laugh."

"My grandaddy told me a tale," said one. "There was a man went travelling to Asia. And he cot a tiger. And it bit him. And after that he went travelling to India. And he cot a snake. And it squeezed him. And after that he went travelling to Americky. And he got a wife. And she bate him. And after that he came home. And he got nothing. And that was the best ever he had."

"That is a foolish story," said the little girl.

"For all," said Keth in her faint voice, "it is better to rest than to be travelling always."

EPILOGUE

The sun crept on around the door. It
lit a picture upon the wall—the picture of
a young girl who stroked a horse with a
white face. It lit the solitary vine, so that
only for this short span it lived, blushing
and radiant.

"I heard a tale that is true," said the
biggest boy. "There was an old one down
the road to-day, saying how she was a great
lady had three houses with golden gates,
and three coloured rings and a dimond
crown. 'I'm the wonder of the North
and West,' said she. And wasn't she only
an ould codger, had the rags hanging about
her the way you'd hang out a hare's pelt
upon a tree!"

"That is an old spent tale," whispered
Keth. "It is grown distant to me as a
song adrift upon the wind."

The sun moved further. It touched the
heads of the children one by one, so that
each was discovered of a different hue, this
one reddish or stained with bronze, this
pale as amber. It touched Keth's face, then
climbed along the wall behind her, lingering
in a pensive square that warmed its hue to
rose.

"And I heard a true story too," said Timmeen proudly. "There is a man that is a Saint rode by this way, looking for the one who is his lady. Going every place he is, saying how he must find her, for he'll be making a queen of her in the Eastern hills."

Keth did not stir. "You told me the best tale of all," she said. Then, because of the sun, she closed her eyes.

"I think," said Timmeen, "you are that lady." And he stroked her hand.

"Of what avail," said Keth. Her voice was so low that they could scarcely hear. "Yet that was a fair tale," she said, "and a dream that is gentle for the edge of sleep."

The children pressed about her. "If you'd fancy him," said they, "will we go send to tell him where you are?"

"It is maybe better to dream," whispered Keth; "and one that will travel his own ways from this out, thinking gently of me, whose company brought him little ease."

The sunlight climbed higher upon the wall, leaving their heads. For a moment it lingered there, and was flushed to a profounder rose. Then, with the leap of a candle, it went out.

"Don't stir now," said Timmeen. "For I think she went asleep."

"We will play a game," said the little girl. "Now let each one of you shut up your eyes, and see who it is will stop so the longest, for that's the way that we'll not waken her."

The little ones screwed up their eyes, and for a full half-minute sat in painful quiet.

A tramping of feet began upon the bridge, as outside, the labourers went by, returning from their work.

From behind the house, the rooks flew westward. Their short wings beat upon the air. Now and again one gave a little squawk. Then they fell silent, and with a brushing sound were gone into the yellow sky.

After a while two gulls came flying from the sea. Their wings were long and tapering. And passing, they made no sound at all.

Then a single step was heard upon the

EPILOGUE

bridge.   While into the untroubled sky cut
a cracked voice:

> "I am the Countess Corrigan
> Of high blood and ancēstry,
> Jewels hanging from me
> Like cobwebs from a rafter.
> If ye'd see a fine knacky sprout
> Of th' ould Irish gintry,
> Look at me now!
> And take off your hats from your heads."

THE END

Milton Keynes UK
Ingram Content Group UK Ltd.
UKHW042319190224
438117UK00001B/1